BONES

HEARTBREAKER MC #2

ALEXIS ABBOTT

PATHFORGERS PUBLISHING

Get an EXCLUSIVE book, **FREE** just as a thank you for signing up for my newsletter! Plus you'll never miss a new release, cover reveal, or promotion!

http://alexisabbott.com/newsletter

PART OF THE HEARTBREAKERS MC
SERIES

Reading Order:

Don't miss out on the rest of the Heartbreakers Series by Alexis Abbott!

> *Breaker*
> *Bones*
> *Ironside*
> *Big Daddy*

I feel the force ripple up from my rough, cracked knuckles through my tattooed forearm and thick bicep as my fist finds its mark right where I want it, smack in the middle of the asshole's nose and send him half-sprawled against the bar and into the people next to him. He's a big guy, and he nearly knocks the other customers over, but I don't care. I'm seeing red.

And this fucker is gonna be spitting red by the time I'm done with him.

"Get up!" I bark down at him as he stares up at me wide-eyed probably still seeing stars instead of the biker about to knock him the fuck out. "What's the matter, fuckhead? Didn't bring enough roofie for me too? Am I too much man for you?"

The guy looks up at me, and I can almost see the gears in his mind turning as he realizes that I am in fact the leather-clad biker who just socked him in the face.

"You hear me?" I shout, rolling my shoulders back and straightening my kutte before I roll my shoulders back. "Get on your fuckin' feet, I'm not about to fight a man on the ground."

It was around eleven o'clock last time I checked the time at a bar in a middle-of-nowhere town called Pine Haven, Wyoming. Outside, the sky is silent and clear, the stars are beautiful, and the air is clean. Inside, the smell of stale smoke is hanging in the air, the sound of harsh music is thrumming from an old jukebox with its glass broken, and the whole bar is getting riled up as I stand back and the guy I just threw down with puts a hand on the bar to pull himself up.

"Hey hey hey, take this shit outside!" Eli the bartender tries to shout, and he reaches over the bar to put a hand on the shoulder of the guy I punched.

But the guy shakes his shoulder away from the bartender and stands up to his full height, and he is most definitely looking *down* at me. Considering how tall I am, that's impressive. The rest of the bar has directed its attention squarely to us by now. This bar isn't exactly the kind of place you go looking for a fight, but it has its rough edges. About five seats' worth of people have gotten up from their places at the bar to give us a wide berth. Most of them look a little surprised that a fight is breaking out so suddenly, but none of them look too bent out of shape about it either.

The one person acting differently is the girl behind the big guy—the girl whose drink I saw him about to drug. The evidence is still sitting on the bar just inches from her drink, right where his hand was before I yanked him back and showed him what I thought about that. I barely had a chance to get a good look at her, and I still don't, but one glimpse past his shoulder is all I need to make eye contact, and that's all the time I need to know she's the most beautiful thing I've ever laid eyes on.

All this happened in a matter of seconds, and each one feels like an hour. The fucker I decked must be able to see straight again, because his face turns red, and he lunges with a blow that just barely misses my ear as I dodge him to the right, letting him bowl past my body and stumble past me as I jeer at him from behind.

"Come on, big guy, how were you gonna get your girl home when you're that far gone?" I quip, laughing at the man to get him good and pissed off.

On top of being big and burly, even by my standards, the guy has a pretty damn classically handsome face, to boot. He isn't a biker, that much is for sure. He's not wearing a kutte, and he's dressed a little too nice for this place, just enough to tell me he isn't a regular. Of course he isn't a regular. Bastard probably wouldn't risk drugging girls at his regular watering hole. If I have my way, he'll be drinking through a straw the rest of his life anyway, so it won't matter.

"You just made a big mistake," he says in that stiff voice that barely contains the anger boiling under the surface.

I know that tone. It comes from a very rigorous kind of conditioning, and the guy's buzz cut and stiff posture all make sense now. This guy has military training, I have no doubt about it. And is that about to stop me from tearing him a new asshole?

Nah.

"You're the one with the bloody nose, boss," I said, putting my fists up and getting ready for him.

He didn't like that much.

To the guy's credit, he was no novice. When he came in again, he didn't do anything stupid like pull his arm back to give me a good idea of where the punch was coming from or leave a limb too exposed for me to catch. But I had gone toe to toe with some of the meanest sons of bitches on this side of the Rockies.

He had also been drinking, and that meant all that fancy military hand-to-hand combat training was on training wheels. When he comes back for more, he isn't nearly as clean and tactical. He tries to grab me, and like most bar fights do, ours ends up staggering aside as we struggle against each other. My arms are busy keeping his off me, but he gets one of his free long enough to throw a punch that catches me across my jaw.

In return, I tighten my grip on his shirt and pull him closer so that I can crack that very same spot on his bleeding nose with my thick forehead.

"Fuckin' Christ!" he shouts as he covers his nose, and when I see the whites of his eyes again, they're showing furious red veins.

He growls as he barrels toward me again, and this time, I have to receive all however-many-hundreds of pounds of this guy there is as it pushes me back into the barstools. As I go back, I catch myself on the bar with one hand, and I throw a quick jab that catches his eye with the other fist. In the split second that buys me, I reach out and grab his collar in an iron grip.

Also in that split second, I catch the sound of the bartender shouting over the phone, which means security is on its way, which means I need to wrap this up quick.

I've got the guy's collar in my hand, so I put it to use. Using it like a real collar, I yank him down into the barstools, sending his whole frame crashing into the mess of iron bars and sticky, beer-coated concrete. As soon as he's down, I pause and watch him for a moment.

Any respectable man would know that was the end, but I was right to listen to my gut. I see his hand shoot into his jacket's inner pocket. I am not about to wait around and find out what he's going to pull out of there. Too many men have gotten knives in their ribs with that kind of good faith, or worse.

Without another thought, I reach for the nearest beer bottle and don't even spend time lifting it high over my head. I just clutch it by the neck and smash it to pieces over the guy's head, right on top of it.

Foamy amber liquid flows over his face and washes some of the blood off as his eyes lose their focus, and he mumbles before falling back onto the pile of fallen stools. His hand is still in his pocket. I stare down at him to make sure he's down, breathing heavily and feeling adrenaline ripple through my body.

It's an old friend of mine.

In the last few seconds of silence I have before the bar realizes that the show's over, my eyes drift up toward the set of eyes I feel watching my kutte from behind, and I see her.

I see legs too long to need the red pumps they're wearing, and a black miniskirt much too small for 'em, for that matter. And that suits me just fine, almost as much as the slim leather jacket over her shoulders, far too clean to fit in with the rest of its kind at this bar. She's wearing a red blouse with a zipper down the front, and that tells me exactly what kind of time she's here for.

The look in her smoky eyes does an even better job at that, too. Those cherry-red lips are faintly parted, icy blue eyes wide as she stares at me with more interest than I figure I've ever been looked at by someone who wasn't about to try to kill me. Then again, with this chick, I wouldn't rule that out. There's something in those eyes beyond just gratitude.

But I don't have time to find out what just yet.

"I'm about to get asked to leave," I finally say to her as I take out a $50 and lay it on the bar. "Got friends here, or do you want a walk to your car?"

"I think I'd rather take a walk with you," she says, hardly missing a beat.

We stare at each other for a moment, trying to figure each other out. At last, I give a single nod, and I nod to the door for her to follow as I stride out, not giving so much as a second glance back to the crowd or the jarhead I just knocked out.

Cool, dry air greets us as we step outside, and I rub my chin to check for damage. As I do, the girl in the jacket hurries up to my side and looks at me with worry, then gets in front of me to stop me.

"Did he get you?" she asks, putting her hands up toward me and trying to look at my face in the light. "Are you hurt?"

"What?" I ask, furrowing my brow. "No, are you kidding? Are *you* okay? You saw what he almost did to you, didn't you?"

"Yeah, yeah I did," she says, reaching up and clutching a strand of the golden hair making that outfit look so good. "And...no, I-I'm not," she breathes. "Can I get a ride home?"

What the hell does that mean?

I can't shake the feeling that there's something going on with this girl, but my mind is too out of sorts to try to figure out what. She looks shaken now that I can see her in proper light, but there's still that *something else* behind her eyes. Doesn't matter right now. All that does is that this girl needs to get taken care of, and that's what I plan on doing.

"Of course," I say, stepping around her and heading toward my ride. "All I've got is my bike, though—that a problem for you?"

I come to a stop at my black motorcycle, its sleek body gleaming in the light coming from the porch of the bar. She swallows, and I see the faintest blush cross her cheeks before she nods her head quickly and approaches me. We don't say much as she gets on. I think she's too dazed by everything to get her thoughts together. She keeps looking back at me, but she doesn't protest as I show her how to sit behind me on the bike before I fire it up.

I feel her gasp as the engine roars to life, but then I feel her grip around my torso tighten, and I head off into the night. It's not exactly how I planned on ending this night, but I'm not about to turn my nose up at it.

"Where do you live?" I shout over my shoulder as we start rolling out of town.

"I don't live in town," she calls. "Take the next right, I'll point you!"

I nod, and we're off.

The girl isn't kidding about not living in town. When I first saw her, I guessed she might be someone's granddaughter, or maybe a tourist passing through who happened to just be unlucky. That clearly isn't the case. It's about twenty minutes of riding into the hills before she says that we're close, and at last, she leads me down to a cute little house nestled away out of sight...with no neighbors in sight.

"You're not alone out here, are you?" I ask as we come to a stop at the curb, and I look over my shoulder at her.

I fully expect her to say *no* regardless of the truth, because it didn't occur to me until too late that a guy like me asking a girl like her if she's alone out in the middle of nowhere might be unsettling. But a blush crosses her cheeks, and she hasn't let her hands fall away from my torso yet.

"Yeah, I am," she says, halfway between sounding matter-of-fact and being unable to believe she's saying the words. "Hey, I know this is weird, but do you...want to come in for a drink?"

It takes me all of one second to decide to reply, "Yes ma'am, I do."

As we make our way toward the door, I can't tear my eyes off her ass as she walks ahead of me. I don't know how to make heads or tails of this girl. But from the outfit to the attitude, she knows what she wants, and I like that. She might be a new face, but she's no tourist, that's for damn sure. Maybe it's the adrenaline, but I could swear there's more sway to those hips than there needs to be.

She unlocks the door, and we step into a quaint living room that I barely get a chance to look at before she shuts it behind me again and looks up at me. She brushes a strand of hair out of her face and gets her first real good look at me in the light, and she's about as transfixed as I am with her. And then that spark in her eyes clicks in my mind. I know what it is.

It's barely restrained desire, long held back and long bubbling under the surface, desperate for a place to breach. And as I recognize it, those deep blue eyes know, and she pushes on ahead with what she's wanted to say since we first stepped out of that bar.

"Thanks for what you did back there," she says. "You didn't have to do that. And you could have gotten...well, it could have been really bad," she says, not wanting to think about what might have happened if I lost that fight.

"Don't mention it," I say, shaking my head softly. "Not about to let some fucker do that to anyone."

I want to ask her what she was doing with him in the first place, why they were talking, and whether she had any idea that was going to happen. None of the answers matter right now, though. She casts a quick glance around the living room, and I'm not sure, but I feel like I can recognize a moment's hesitation. Is she having second thoughts about inviting this big, scary biker into her home? Did she get a look at my kutte and see the devil skewering a heart and decide to back out? That isn't what's written in her eyes when she looks back up to mine, but I have to be sure.

"But let me ask you this," my voice growls as I step forward and look down at her. "What's a little slip of a thing like you doing, living out here all alone and going to biker bars?"

What I mean to ask is why she's looking for trouble. And she knows it. The way she looks up at me, you'd think I was her father catching her misbehaving. Maybe that's why her cheeks are burning.

"I don't want to talk about that," she says softly, putting a brave hand on my chest. "What I want is to thank you."

She pushes herself up as high as those heels will send her, and she presses a warm kiss to my lips that makes the half-mast shaft bulging through my pants get hard as a rock.

I have never felt this before.

Every faintest touch of this handsome stranger's fingertips across my body feels like spirals of fire and electricity spreading out like stormy skies beneath the soft porcelain of my skin. I have spent so many long years in hiding, in silence, biding my time and watching from a safe distance. Always at a distance. Always from afar. I never even knew touch could feel like this. Like fire and ice. Like fear and hope and guilt and deep, abiding pleasure all rolled into one potent formula that makes my heart race. I can feel the blood pumping faster through my veins, rushing in my ears. My face feels warm and flushed, and I know in the dim light he can probably still see the rosy tinge to my cheeks and forehead. I wonder, if I were to pull away from his earth-shattering kiss and look down, would I see that my body is blooming rosy, too? It feels like I should be afraid. Like I should be ripping apart at the seams. This is wrong. Every part of this feels like sin, but god, it feels like heaven, too.

And how is a girl like me supposed to tell the difference?

After all, I know better than anyone else how terrifying it can be living in a feminine body. I know what dark depths a man can be pushed to in search of the thing that turns him on. I know how easily pleasure can border on pain, pain on torture, torture on captivity.

Captivity can edge along with camaraderie. A cage can feel like an ivory tower when it's built by the right hands. I've heard of Stockholm syndrome. I've read all about it, just another shadowy corner of my past to sweep and air out, to plumb like a bee seeking nectar. A girl seeking truth. Understanding. I want to make sense of the things that have happened to me and around me. I want to hold the truth in my hands, turn it over and over until my fingertips have memorized every jagged edge. I have to dive into the dark side. Living in the light has only kept me safe in so far as my body. But my heart aches for more. For adventure. For passion.

I yearn for these things which fester far down in my soul, that I rarely give breath to in the silent privacy of my own thoughts, much less ask for. I am not totally naive, though I am fully aware of the fact that every aspect of my face, my hair, my soft body and coquettish smile, all spells naiveté. I'm a human doily. Something delicate and fragile to look at, to hardly touch except to change hands. Sometimes I have thought of myself as one of those dust-collecting tchotchkes on an antique store shelf, eyes pleading, mouth sealed shut, yearning to be bought and sold because then at least I might belong to someone other than myself.

I know what people think when they see me. I get it. Especially if it's a man looking my way. My looks indicate a life of shelter, years spent barely daring to peek beyond the lacy white curtains that hang and flutter over the bay window in my bedroom upstairs. Trust me. When you've seen the things I've seen, when you've walked unknowingly through someone else's nightmare without even noticing at first, you learn first and foremost to protect yourself. When you see how bad things can be, it's only a reflex to close yourself off against it. That has always been my instinct. Recoil. Refuse. Walk away. Go back to the ivory tower where nothing can touch me and therefore nothing can hurt me.

But I knew this day would come.

I know that there is something in me that draws the darkness out. Maybe I even create it myself somehow, unknowingly. Maybe I'm the bad one.

Maybe the evil is in my veins, pumping alongside the scarlet blood and the white-hot adrenaline.

Maybe it's why I'm here right now, folding like a ragdoll into this dark-eyed man's embrace. Like I've been waiting all my life to be held this way. And haven't I? For all my hiding and all my safekeeping, I have never been able to fully kill the ghost. Now his hands are on my body, tangling in my hair, brushing it back from my rosy-cheeked face. His lips are soft and sensual but hard at the same time, and I can't help but wonder if he can feel the softness of mine when he kisses me so hard. Does he see me the way I see me?

Does he see me the way my father saw me?

I wonder if there's anything else to even look at but that. Am I just an echo of him? Am I a facsimile of man's weakness, just another ingénue to be downed like a shot of tequila and washed away with next morning's water. Right now, I don't really care. Or at least, I am trying very hard not to. I have to give this mystery man some credit, though. He makes it easier to forget. When he touches me just right, when he kisses me so hard and so delirious that stars burst and glow under my eyelids, I can almost imagine it's all okay. He's one hell of a distraction from the darkness. But his hands are roving down the narrow slope of my ribcage and my waist. His fingertips press needfully into the hook of my hips. He is melding into me now, our bodies twisting and writhing against each other. I wish I knew what the next step was. I wish I knew how to dance this dance.

At least there's one thing I know for certain: this man has the dance memorized by heart. And if I stand on his feet, he can carry me through the dance. Hell, he can carry me anywhere. Up to the edge and over it. Into the whirling abyss below us, yawning like a great mouth to swallow me whole if I don't cling to him hard enough. He's my lifeboat. He's my anchor.

And I don't even know his name.

"I don't," I murmur breathlessly when he pulls away for a moment. His wolfish eyes bore into mine. I see the fire building there. The ember catching flame.

"I don't know your name," I manage to choke out. My words feel thin and threadbare in the stark, cool air. The only warmth is crackling between us.

A twitch of a devilish smile tugs at the corner of his mouth, but darts away.

"Is that what you want, little girl?" he growls, leaning close so that his hot breath tickles against the sensitive shell of my ear. "You want to be touched by a man whose name you don't even know?"

My breath catches in my throat as he lets his hands slide around to grope my ass. My eyelids flutter, my lips falling open in a pleased sigh. I shrug off my black jacket and it slumps to the floor behind me, unneeded.

"Yes. Yes, that is what I want," I whisper, almost more to myself than to him.

"There's much more to you than meets the eye, isn't there?" he hisses.

In this moment, I feel almost as though he can look right through me.

I'm made of glass. Just as transparent. Just as fragile. Just as coveted.

"I guess it depends on who's looking," I mumble back.

I'm surprised at how easily the words come to me. But then again, I've been dreaming of this moment for years. Maybe not in this exact form. But I knew it would happen eventually. I knew someone would touch me like this if I dared to leave the door open for it.

"And if I'm the one looking?" he hisses. "How does it feel to have a man like me looking at you, sweetheart? Does it feel good?"

"Yes. It feels good," I admit, barely audibly.

"Does it scare you?" he asks.

I bite my lip. "Yes. It scares me," I tell him.

"Do you want to stop?" he presses me, but I can tell by the slight curl of his lip that he already knows the answer. It's written all over my face, I'm sure.

I shake my head ever so slightly. "No. Please don't stop," I beg of him.

"Good girl. That's what I like to hear," he snarls.

His hand slips up to cup my soft, sloping jaw. His hands are so huge that he could easily fit them around my neck. Maybe even just one of them could wrap around. I imagine it over and over again, unable to stop the flood of desirous images. His fingers, thick and calloused from what must be years of manual labor and hard living, perfectly circling my delicate neck. Pressing into my throat. Making me see bright stars bursting in the blackness of my tight-shut eyes.

He could break me without even trying. Hell, he could snap me by accident.

But it's too late to shy away now. I said yes. I *mean* yes. Come what may.

The mysterious stranger scoops me up into his strong arms and lifts me off my feet. An old sensory memory flashes into my laid-bare mind: my father's arms, wide and tensing, lifting me up out of my chair and carrying me, sleepy-headed and lolling, down the hallway to my old childhood bedroom. As my handsome guest cradles me back onto the sofa, I can almost imagine my father's bearded face hovering above me. His thick eyebrows always knitted close together as though in deep contemplation. Like he knew with every moment of his waking life that his fantasies were too dark and ugly to be compatible with my existence in the world.

He lived a double life. I was part of the surface

life. I ran and sang and played in the light while she, that girl whose face looked so painfully like mine, paced and wept and waited in the darkness underneath the facade of our happy home. I have learned, if nothing else, to expect the unexpected. To never trust a smiling face. You never really know what might be lurking in the shadows behind it, relying on your ready willingness to accept that things can be good, that people can be good. I know as well as I know my own name that there is no living creature on this planet more tempted by evil than man.

My name is Lauren Lockett. I have seen the dark side. I have touched it with my own hands. I would recognize it even with my eyes closed. And what this man has burning inside of him is dark, for sure. I can sense it, simmering just under the surface. I wonder: will I be the girl to unlock it and set it free?

My body unfolds for him, opening like a morning glory worshipping the sun. He can take whatever he wants from me. I give it willingly. For better or for worse.

"What *do* you want, angel?" he growls. "Do you even know?"

I open my eyes, noticing for the first time the thin glimmering sheen of crystalline tears clinging to my lashes. I don't know why. Is it only fear? As if fear isn't enough. I start to turn my head away, averting my eyes. It's too hard to look at him head-on, even in the low light of the full moon glowing dimly through the lacy curtains. But he doesn't want me to do that. He takes my chin in one hand, tracing my bottom lip. The other hand slides around to cup the back of my head. He turns me back to face him and I tremble in his grasp even as I accept.

"Answer me. Look me in the eyes and answer me," he commands.

I know better than to deny a man like him.

"I want you to tell me what to do," I tell him genuinely. "I need you to guide me."

"You're dancing around it," he points out, and he's right. I am.

I tug at his leather jacket and press a soft kiss to his thumb against my lip.

"I want less talking," I admit to him.

He grins and dives in to kiss me again, harder this time. More passionately. It's not quite desperation, but it borders on it. I know he's pulled back like a rubber band, like an arrow in the quivering bow. He's trying to hold back, but only barely. His hands grope their way down my body, squeezing and caressing my breasts through the thin fabric of my blouse. He pulls at the hem and I instinctively lift my arms so he can tear the red crop top off of me. I hear him inhale sharply at the reveal of my bare chest. I'm not wearing a bra. It was an intentional choice. My nipples stiffen to peaks as he toys with my breasts, feeling them up as his lips move against mine, crashing harder and more insistent with every inch of clothing he peels away from my body. He tugs down my black skirt and tosses it aside while I kick off my red stiletto pumps. He rears back and drops his own jacket before unbuttoning his jeans. I watch, my eyes wide and my chest rising and falling hard with every labored breath, as he lets his massive cock bounce free in the brisk air of my little hideaway house. I can't help but lick my lips, my mouth watering at the sight of his shaft. He stands up and snaps his fingers.

"Sit up. Look at me. Touch yourself," he orders gruffly.

I follow directions dutifully. I pull myself up into a sitting position, staring at him, my eyes riveted to his gaze while my hands trail down my shivering naked body to my warm, fragrant sex between my thighs. I groan as my own fingers dance around my sensitized clit. My mysterious stranger watches me, his hand sliding up and down his cock languidly. I tilt my head back and start to relax, the pleasurable sensations melting through me. I begin to roll my hips, touching myself while he watches. His eyes feel like two beams of bright light on my body. I can feel every flick of his glance like a hit to the chest. I'm embarrassed, but it feels good somehow. I don't feel ashamed. I know I probably should, though. Does that make me just as bad?

Maybe that's the real truth. I've been running from the past because I never wanted it to look like me. But maybe it looks more like I do than I ever expected. This man is bringing me to the mirror and forcing me to look. I'm afraid and aroused in nearly equal measure, but desire is swiftly rising up to overwhelm the fear, especially as my fingertips massage tight, delicious circles around my clit. Just as I'm about to climax, I work myself back from the edge. I'm not ready to give in just yet. Not to my own pleasures.

I have so much I want to give away, but I don't know the way.

"I want to make you feel good. Tell me what to do," I plead softly.

He seems to figure it out; that I don't know what I'm doing. He doesn't shy away from it. Instead, he takes me by both shoulders and moves me from the sofa to the floor.

"On your knees for me," he growls roughly. I kneel, looking up at him expectantly.

Like a repentant aching for the taste of wafer-thin forgiveness.

When he moves closer and his cock throbs in front of my face, instinct takes over. I lean forward, first gently licking the end of his cock to taste the shiny bead of precum glistening there. He cups the back of my head, pushing me closer. I pull the full length of his cock into my warm, wet mouth inch by inch. I revel in the new sensation of my cheeks aching to accommodate his size. He groans low in his throat and his hips snap forward almost involuntarily, thrusting down my throat. I start to gag at first, but I manage to maintain my composure. I flick my eyes up to look at his gorgeous, sharp-featured face while I bob up and down on his cock. I move back and forth, swallowing down his salty precum as he grabs my head with both huge hands. He holds me in place while he rears back and slams down my throat again and again and again. I suck his cock harder, my own body tingling with desire as I lick and suck him closer and closer to the brink.

"So good for me, little girl," he growls.

I moan, sending little thrums of vibration up through his body while he thrusts in and out of my mouth. He's stiffening and tensing with every movement. I've never wanted anything more than the taste of his honey in my throat. I suck harder, taking down every precious inch of his glorious cock eagerly. He fucks my mouth, his hips pistoning in and out as he starts to lose control. His fingers tangle in my hair and hold me still. He seizes up and groans, goosebumps prickling up on his skin as his cock spurts hot, sticky seed down my throat. I cough a little but immediately, enthusiastically suck down every gorgeous drop.

Pure elation floods my body and I lean back, letting his cock slip out of my mouth with a wet, resounding pop. I lick my lips and slowly stand up, a coy smile on my swollen lips. This is exactly what

I've been craving. Everything I have been too afraid to reach for. He's perfect. This night is perfect.

But just as I stand up, before I can say another word, the blood rushes out of my head and my vision starts to go dark and starry. My heart slows. I can't clench my hands. My body is weak and I fall, crumpling like a tower of paper to the floor as the world goes black.

BONES

I can't remember the last time I felt this way. I feel like I'm glowing, and every muscle in my body feels refreshed at a deep, almost cellular level. Every second she was around me felt like bliss, and when I turn my head to watch her get up, I feel my insides get all warm and fuzzy at the sight of that ass and the way her hips—

"Shit," I curse as I see her start to wobble on her feet in a way I know all too well.

I jump up off the couch in time for her limp weight to fall back my arms. I catch her with one hand supporting the space between her shoulders and the other holding her at the hips, and effortlessly, I lift her up bridal-style and stare down at the blank, unconscious non-expression on her face.

She's out cold, no doubt about it. I grit my teeth and look around the apartment, wondering what the odds are she really does have any roommates that are just holed up in their rooms hiding. But no, I know on a gut level she was being honest. We're alone out here, and this house is just me, my bike, and a passed-out girl who just gave me the best oral I've had in my life. She's needed my help twice tonight, but she's more than made it up, as far as I'm concerned.

"Shit, girl, did you take a sip of that drink anyway while you were enjoying the show?" I murmured to her under my breath as I carried her toward the hallway, peeking down it for a light switch.

Seeing one, I awkwardly turn and walk sideways down the hallway, flicking on the light. I almost pause for a moment, because the light floods the narrow passage and shows me the handful of picture frames hanging up.

They're all landscape pictures.

I recognize a few of them from the local area, but there's a striking absence of people in any of the pictures in the hallway. No family, no friends, none of her. I don't waste time trying to make heads or tails of that information. I check the first door and find a small closet, and the second is a bathroom. That leaves the third door at the end of the hall, and that door swings open to reveal a tidy master bedroom.

I flick the light on and carry her inside, and I'm grateful it looks like she didn't make the bed this morning before getting up and going. I don't have any free hands, so I have to slide her in legs-first and lay her on her back before folding her hands over her stomach and pulling the blankets over her gently.

Once she's tucked in as well as I can manage, I stand back and look down at her. I suddenly realize I should feel like an intruder here, but I don't. Her head falls to the side, facing me, and her features look more peaceful and relaxed than I've ever seen in a sleeping woman before. I watch her chest rising and falling with her steady, tranquil breaths, and every one of those breaths makes the soft curls of her blonde hair flicker beside her in the moving air. She's naked, and I've only known her for about an hour, if that.

It's just me and this woman who gets more interesting every minute I spend with her, out in the middle of nowhere. A lesser man might take advantage of the situation, and I've gotta say, I'm glad I'm the one out of all the bikers in that bar who saved her ass from that chickenshit rapist.

I take a moment to look around the room, and I have to admit, I'm not someone who lives extravagantly or who'd know "contemporary tastes" if they hit me in the face, but the room looks remarkably simple. She looks about the age that she might be a student, but the only colleges around here aren't the kind you come in from out of county to attend, much less out of state. And I definitely haven't seen this girl around, so I can only imagine she blew into town recently.

Then again, this is the kind of place you stay if you want to get away from the world, not live neck-deep in it like you'd think a twenty-something young woman would be doing. But this woman isn't like most. That much is becoming clear, I just can't put my finger on the how or why.

Once she's tucked in and decent under the covers, I make my way back through the hallway into the kitchen. I stop at the closet to poke my head in, and after a quick search, I find a small hand towel that feels freshly washed and folded. She lives neatly, whoever she is.

I take it into the kitchen, find a bag of frozen peas in the freezer, dust the freezer burn off, and wrap the cloth around it before rinsing it in cold water to make a cold compress. It isn't much, but it's better than nothing, and it might help in combination with an aspirin.

Why the girl fainted is still a mystery to me. My best guess is that she had too much to drink and just managed to hide it somehow until the excitement on the couch got to be too much for her. I sigh and look around the room, noting how simple and unlived-in the house looks, furrowing my brow. Or maybe this girl just escaped some kind of crazy repressed family, and she's trying to throw herself headlong into as much vice as she can handle. Going from zero to having your lips wrapped around a biker's cock after almost getting roofied would be overwhelming to anyone.

But girls who just got out from under an oppressive wing don't dress like this girl is dressed. She knows what she's doing, at least to some degree. I don't have a wilting flower on my hands. I can sense the thorns on this rose a mile away, she just hasn't shown them yet.

Rummaging around her kitchen doesn't yield any aspirin. She must keep it somewhere besides the kitchen. Not wanting to let the cold compress start to melt, I make my way back to the bedroom and find her right where I left her, still dozing peacefully. It's like she laid down for a portrait, her body looks so picturesque. I sit down beside her and check her pulse to make sure nothing is seriously wrong, and when that feels fine, I press the ice to her forehead.

After a few minutes of watching her like that, I start searching the room for aspirin. Maybe it's in a nightstand or a dresser. Even though she's out cold, I move carefully and quietly, because I don't want her to wake up and panic at the sight of a biker who's a head taller than her rummaging through her underwear drawer.

The first drawer is just folded shirts, and the second I slide open looks like storage for either important documents or junk mail she hasn't gotten around to sorting through and throwing out yet. Sure, that might be just me projecting why I have a huge stack of unopened mail in a drawer at my place, but you never know.

I wish I could say I'm looking for aspirin when I reach down to push some of the envelopes aside, but honestly, I'm being nosy. I want to see if I can catch her last name. I already know this girl is worth trying to stay in touch with, if she still wants that when she wakes up. And something in my gut is still telling me there's more to this woman than meets the eye.

It almost makes me feel more guilty when my curiosity pays off.

As soon as I push the top layer of mail out of the way, I lay eyes on a newspaper clipping that looks aged as hell. I glance at the date at the top, which she —assuming she's the one who clipped the newspaper —went out of her way to preserve. It's dated over a decade ago. I don't know her exact age, but she can't have been more than a young girl that long ago, or a teenager at most. And that gets my attention only because of what the headline on the article itself says:

"Child Abducted by Wyoming Man Found Safe!"

Glimpses of the article give more details. A twelve year old girl found kidnapped and chained up by a man old enough to be a father. The implications of something terrible happening to her, or about to have happened to her. It wasn't clear at the time they ran this article, and they probably wanted to respect the poor girl's privacy. But with this timeline...I glance back at the slumbering form on the bed and furrow my brow.

There's no way the woman passed out on the bed right now is the same girl from this news story who suffered so much at such a young age, is there?

"Christ," I murmur, sliding the drawer shut.

Before it closes, I see the woman's name on a piece of junk mail: Lauren Lockett. I silently mouth the name and feel my heart rate pick up briefly. It's a pretty name. Real pretty. I'm a simple man, but I appreciate the little things like that. *Lauren Lockett.* It's more whimsical and innocent than the leather-clad bombshell seems, but it suits her, somehow.

I pull my phone out to text Breaker. I can't find any aspirin, but it just hit me that the rush of the past hour probably has the rest of the MC wondering where the fuck I am. Well, they can probably figure it out, but I went and ruined their night by doing what I did.

The rest of my motorcycle club—the Wyoming Heartbreakers, whose kutte I'll proudly wear until the day I die—was playing pool when I started that fight. They weren't involved, and even though I didn't check on them when I was in the middle of the fight, I don't think they would have gotten in the way unless the would-be rapist had buddies with him to outnumber me.

We Heartbreakers like a fair fight.

The texts are about what I'd expect: mostly wondering where the fuck I am, and letting me know that they all rode back to the clubhouse after I left. I chuckle at the way some of the guys phrase it, but I go straight to Breaker's messages first to touch base with him.

Hey Prez. Had to get the girl home. Taking care of her. Anything happen after I left? Asshole not dead is he?

It's only a second before I hear back, which tells me the guys are probably at the clubhouse already, having a few drinks and gossiping about whether I fought well with that asshole. At least, I'd like to think that's what they're doing, and that they're not all hanging out in county jail if that bartender called the cops. But biker bartenders are usually alright about fights, so I'm not sweating it. I make my way back to the bedside, taking a seat on it carefully as I carry on the rest of the conversation.

His ego's bruised, says Breaker. **He was military, bartender said locals love him. Might be some blowback. You sure he was trying to drug her, brother?**

POSITIVE. Girl can back me up. Saw the powder on the counter, so did the bartender.

Hey I believe you, just giving heads up. How's the girl?

She was fine for a while, til she passed out. Keeping an eye on her. Did you see her drink any of the spiked drink?

No, not after you punched the guy at least. Doesn't make sense, she'd have been loopy earlier.

See her drinking at all?

No

I furrow my brow and look down at Lauren, worried.

"Damn, girl, are you just sick?" I murmur as I text Breaker once more to let him know I'll probably be staying the night but that I'll keep them posted, and I thank the MC for cleaning up after me. Breaker doesn't mind me doing what I did. He expects us to watch out for people who can't watch out for themselves. That's what the Heartbreakers are about, and that's not changing anytime soon.

I reach down and brush some hair out of the girl's face and pull some of the sheets further up her collar, covering her a little more uniformly. I can't get over how serene she looks, and it makes me wish I had more to offer her. But the nearest store is a gas station miles away, and by the time I'd get back from a run like that, she'd be alone almost a full hour, and I don't feel good about that. Not right now, at least. For all I know, Mr. Military Hero might have her address.

But just five minutes of peaceful silence later, I hear a soft murmur from her, and I look away from my phone down at her and see her starting to stir ever so faintly. Her eyes crack open, and as she stares up at the ceiling in the brief moment before all her senses and memories come back to her...I see deep emptiness in those eyes.

She's awake, and after a moment of watching her chest rising and falling at a different rate, I can tell it hasn't taken her long to come to. After the initial sadness in her expression passes, her eyes flutter open, and then she gasps at the sight of me looming over her. I hold up my hands inoffensively as she clutches her chest, but then she recognizes me, and I see the fear replaced with a sudden blush as memory floods back to her.

She even cracks a smile, which touches me so much that I can't help but return it. That wasn't the reaction I was expecting from a girl waking up to the sight of me.

"Hey," my husky voice says in the dim light of the room.

"Hey," she replies, just before a soft, embarrassed laugh. "Um...god, I'm sorry," she murmurs, rubbing her eyes.

"I'm just gonna keep saying 'don't mention it' until you get the message," I chuckle, shaking my head.

"What even happened?" she asks, noticing the

cold pack on her head and putting it aside on the nightstand. "Wait, was that you?"

"I was hoping you'd be able to answer that," I say, scratching my head. "And yeah, hope you weren't planning on using those peas for anything important. I just got you to bed and wrapped that up for you in case it was a hangover hitting early. Should I take you to the hospital? My ride's got plenty of gas in it."

At this point, she's rubbing her face more to save herself the embarrassment of looking back up at me, but the gratitude in her eyes when she does look at me is radiant as it is obvious.

"No, no, I'm good," she says, smiling. "But thank you. I just feel bad for keeping you here all night."

"Hey, you can keep me here as long as you like," I tease, giving her a gruff grin that makes her blush satisfyingly before my expression grows more serious. "You...remember all that, too?"

"Yeah, that's all pretty clear, don't worry," she says, smile growing as she gives a more sincere laugh that puts my nerves at ease. "I...needed that, after that kind of night out."

"Look who's talking," I laugh, squeezing her hand, and she squeezes it back as our eyes go lidded. "And hey, I'll beat it if you really want, but I'd feel better hanging out here tonight in case that asshole from the bar happened to tail us. We'd probably know by now, but just in case. I think I saw some blankets in the closet, I can crash on the couch."

"I'd like that," she says, not letting go of my hand as her tentative, cautious voice speaks against her better judgment. "But I'd like it more if you stayed a little closer," she adds with a faint nod toward the other side of the bed.

I'd be out of my mind to say no, even if my cock weren't already starting to swell in anticipation. I stare down at her with a hundred questions on my mind. Who the hell is she? Why does she have that article in her drawer? Is this place as much of a safe-house as it looks like? What the fuck was I getting myself into?

But right then, there was only one response either of us wanted to hear from my lips.

"That sounds great."

Trying to sleep that night would have been a joke, plain and simple. It was no surprise to me to learn that Lauren is a cuddler. As soon as I got out of my clothes and into bed with her, she was up against my side, and brother, it's hard to sleep when your cock is as thick as it was with her lips wrapped around it all night. She rests her head against me, and I feel her body matching the rhythm of my heartbeat as she drifts off to sleep in short order.

That leaves me to stare at the ceiling and wonder just what this girl's story must be.

My senses have been telling me from the moment I saw the look in her eyes at me beating that guy's ass that something is off. I don't know what, and I'll be the first to admit that it's hard to figure out what when you're busy getting some action from a girl I could spend all night in. But after the third time I almost doze off only to snap back awake, I realize I've got a lot of time to think things over before we have to talk again.

Why would she have that damn newspaper article? That question has been burning brightest at the front of my mind, because I know it's the one that I probably can't ask her directly. If I bring it up, I'll have to explain why I was rummaging through her stuff. Granted, "I was looking for aspirin while you were passed out" is a pretty good excuse if you ask me, but she might not see it that way.

And I can't shake the feeling that I don't want to do anything that would turn this girl sour to me. Even if something doesn't add up about her, I feel like I want her at my back, on the same page as me.

All I can imagine is that she's the girl in the article. If she is, then my heart breaks for her. The idea of being imprisoned by her own father like that sends a rush of anger through me so intense that I worry my heartbeat will wake her up. Part of me wants to get up, go back to the drawer, and see what else that article says. I wonder if the dad ever got locked up like he ought to be.

That would also be a good reason for a girl to be living alone out in the middle of nowhere, Wyoming, too.

I look down at the peacefully slumbering silhouette of Lauren in the darkness. A little light is filtering through the crack of the ensuite bathroom door. She left the light and fan on when she went to the bathroom before dozing off. It's a cute touch I notice, and I have to admit, the bathroom fan is kind of hypnotic after a while when there's nothing else to listen to. Beats the wind outside.

But as her chest rises and falls with each breath, I can't help but wonder what kind of life she's had. My MC and I, we've lived through our share of trauma. When I first met Breaker back when we were members of the club called the Buzzsaws, he killed a man when he found out our old prez was getting into sex trafficking. And years ago, when I first got the hell out of SoCal and headed to the plains, god knows I left my share of trauma long those long, dusty roads.

That's just what life with a kutte is like. But we'll never know the pain that little girl went through. But I'm getting ahead of myself. I don't know for sure they're the same person, and for all I know, she could just be collecting macabre stories as a hobby.

She was dressed for a good time at the bar, so I'm not about to question that, but she didn't act like most of the non-bikers you meet at a biker bar. For starters, she wasn't hanging onto everyone with a kutte she came across, she was talking to that piece of shit I shut down. And he sure as hell wasn't posing as a biker.

Girls who come that close to something bad

happening usually don't want to jump into bed with you that night, in my experience. But me driving her home was entirely her idea, and so was inviting me in, shutting the door, and pressing one hell of a kiss to my lips. There was nothing at *all* wrong with that in my book, but pair that with how she passed out right after oral, and it adds up to a scene that doesn't make a ton of sense.

Maybe it's the lack of sleep at around 4:00 in the morning, but I start to wonder if she has some other kind of motive. Damn, now that I think about it, she did jump into bed with me awfully fast, but con artists are usually more careful than to just let a random biker into their house alone at night, right? I wouldn't have trusted anyone but the other Heartbreakers in that bar to do the same for Lauren.

That couldn't be the point, could it? Does this girl have some kind of death wish?

No, I figure there's something else going on, and I don't like it.

We Heartbreakers have big fish to fry. Ever since we put the Buzzsaws in their place, we've been trying to clean up this side of the state and undo the damage they did. And right now, that task has a face: a mean son of a bitch called Diesel is one of the few members of Buzz's dead club who wasn't accounted for after the smoke cleared, and we can't find him anywhere in the region. The man's a ghost, and there's no way he isn't looking for revenge, or worse, starting up a new operation somewhere.

The clipping in Lauren's dresser reminds me of him. As long as there are men like that guy out there, we can't stop hunting them down like the invasive predators they are. I staked my life on that kind of philosophy long before I even met Breaker and turned my back on Buzz.

Chances are slim, but I wouldn't put it past Diesel to set up a trap.

After all, Diesel knows the Heartbreakers are in this area, and he knows we got our whole start protecting a woman from that kind of thing. A clumsy attempt to drug a girl in front of me would have been easier bait than I'd like to admit. I'd like to think I'd be dead by now if this was a trap, but I can't be sure, and if I get caught, it'd mean a bloody, painful death under torture and questioning.

I'd rather not run the risk of my last sight being Diesel swinging an extension cord's prongs at my face, so I decide it's time to hit the road before she gets up.

Right when I see the first tinge of blue that tells me sunrise is about to begin, I carefully slip out of bed and pull my clothes back on. I take my time so as not to wake her, but she's still and peaceful the whole time I get dressed. As my kutte rests on my shoulders, I decide it's best not to look back at her before I stalk back down the hallway and out the door. As I'm walking across the yard, the sun is finally cresting over the horizon and painting the sky gorgeous colors.

But as I mount my bike, I close my eyes for a moment, and I curse under my breath. She rode here with me, meaning her car was probably back at the bar. I couldn't just strand her at home. My eyes turn to the house once more, and somehow, it's no surprise that I see her pretty little face staring right back at me from her bedroom window.

And there's that haunted, empty look in her eyes again.

It's the same look she wore when she first woke up last night, when she thought she was alone for a moment. My mind goes back to that article as I watch her staring at me impassively. We stare at each other for a few seconds, but her face doesn't change. She doesn't wave to me, doesn't try to beckon me back in, and doesn't give me the finger. She just stares with that hard-to-read look in her eyes.

I give her a nod and a gesture to let her know that I'll be back.

Realistically, what I'll probably do is get round up one of the guys and come back with company to help her get her car. If this is a trap and she's watching me walk out of it, she'll be banking on me coming back alone. And I don't want to get caught with my pants down if that happens.

My engine roars, and I feel her eyes following me

as I ride into the sunrise, heading toward our clubhouse.

The wind whips around my body, and even though my head is fuzzy after a long, sleepless night, the thrill of riding wakes me up like a charm. There's nothing like the freedom of roaring across an open road with a trail of dust behind you and nothing but the same stretching out forever ahead of you. There were a lot of stretches of road out here where all you saw in both directions was road and plains, and that suited me just fine. It did when I blazed across the Mojave, I did it when I was weaving through the mountains of Utah, and it does now. No matter what the land, as long as I'm riding, I feel free.

At least, I usually do. Before long, my mind drifts back to that odd house in the hills, like it's an anchor tying me back and urging me to return. Part of me feels like I'll ride back there with one of my fellow Heartbreakers only to find nothing there, like it was all some strange illusion all along.

I run my hand over my face. Now I *know* it's the lack of sleep talking. But that girl was downright ethereal, and she felt every bit as good as she looked. That's something you don't forget easily, not even when you live a life that never lets you settle down too long.

I pull up at the clubhouse, and I see that the MC's bikes are already lined up outside. Looks like nobody else had a late night. It's about 8:00 in the morning by the time I arrive, and when I stride in, the level of activity is about what I'd expect: nothing.

Ironsides and Big Daddy are hanging out on the ground level, both of them eating some fast food for breakfast.

"Hey hey, Casanova's back," Big Daddy chuckles deeply as I come in and roll my eyes.

Ironsides doesn't say anything, but he gives me that vaguely intimidating smile and nod he knows so well. I can never tell if he means it to look unsettling, but Ironsides might just be a scary looking bastard, good a heart as he's got.

"C'mon, where is she?" Big Daddy asks, leaning forward. "You didn't leave her on your bike, did you? We know you're more of a gentleman than that, Bones."

"We'll get to that," I say, chuckling. "Might have some things to tie up on the business side of last night before we can think about that. Is Breaker around?"

"Downstairs," Ironsides grunts, jabbing a thumb toward the stairs.

"He wants to see you," Big Daddy adds, nodding. "Wouldn't keep him waiting. Sounds like your conversation last night has him worried."

"Good," I say, striding past them and heading down the stairs and murmuring to myself, "It has me worried too."

I head downstairs to what looks like a speakeasy

right out of New York City, all the way up here in Wyoming. This place used to be falling apart, but Breaker bought the place after renting the basement for long enough, and his girl Kate fixed it up better than Breaker could have ever dreamed.

She isn't around today, but that's not unusual. She keeps busy with that baby on the way, no matter how much Breaker tries to keep her safe at home. I make my way past the bar to the meeting room, where I find our prez waiting for me at the end of the conference table.

"Bones," he says as I enter, glancing up at me briefly. "Glad to see you're in one piece. Sounds like everything went alright this morning?"

"We usually don't drill each other like this after a one night stand," I say with a grin, taking a seat close to him at his end of the table. "So I'm guessing that means you're worried about the same thing I am."

"Diesel doesn't need to stop and take a break," Breaker agrees with a deep sigh, reaching for the fast food breakfast I see he cashed in on as well. "See anything suspicious as her at her house?"

He slides a sausage and egg biscuit my way, and I tear into it as soon as I can smell it. I forgot how hungry I am.

"Haven't picked up on anything that's sending off alarm bells," I say. "No urgent ones, at least. Simple house, no pictures, not a lot of personal touches. Need to go back there for her and give her a ride to her car, it's still at the bar. She's hiding from something, or someone, I'd wager."

"Or, she's bait that Diesel set out for one of us to take," Breaker points out, and I'm nodding before he even finishes the thought.

"That's why I got the fuck out of there so early," I say after a mouthful of buttery biscuit. "But I don't think that's the case. I think Diesel's not above it, but she had all the chances in the world she wanted with me. I didn't even sleep last night, and she didn't budge. Nobody with something on their mind like that would sleep that peacefully. I mean, unless she's a trained operative or something, and *that's* something I can't say I can see Diesel pulling off."

"Nah," Breaker agreed, chuckling. "Good point, we'd be in over our heads if we were up against that. Can't let ourselves underestimate him, though. I'm proof enough of what a lone man backed against the wall is capable of. I'm not giving Diesel the same opportunity I took advantage of to kill Buzz." He pauses, then looks at me less seriously. "How was it, by the way?"

I roll my eyes, and Breaker punches my arm as we chuckle.

"Good," I admit. "Damn good. The kind you don't forget, good."

"You're making a strong case for the secret agent angle," Breaker points out casually.

"Hey, nothin' against secret agents as long as they're working for us," I say.

Breaker watches me for a moment with a smile, then gives the nod I know means our meeting is over. He stands up, and I wad up my trash as I follow suit.

"Alright, that's all I wanted to touch base on. Don't worry about the ride, I'll go get her for you. If she acts funny around me, too, it'll tell us whether she's safe. If she's Diesel's, then she'll try to pull something on me. If not, I'll see you back here—to remind you about that money you owe Ironsides from pool," he added.

My instinct is to bristle at the idea of Breaker going to get my girl, but then again, she's not my girl —she's her own. I bite back the childish impulse and nod, walking out with Breaker toward the door.

"Got it. Post up and wait for you to get back and see if we have an agent on our hands," I said.

"And pay Ironsides," Breaker calls, but I'm already halfway up the stairs with a grin on my face.

He'll get that money when I win it back from him.

LAUREN

I can't seem to stop stealing furtive glances over at the man behind the steering wheel of the vintage car. My whole body is still tingling with the newness of it all. Riding in cars with boys. Talking to boys. Letting a boy touch my body.

No. Not a boy, I correct myself. A man. A *real* man.

I stare out the window nervously, the glossy tinted windows nearly perfectly reflecting my anxious, wide-eyed expression. I'm grinding my teeth, my fingertips tapping out a frenetic involuntary rhythm on the inner door handle. I know, somehow vaguely, that this must be a little annoying for my gracious chauffeur to listen to, but I can't seem to make myself stop. I feel packed to the brim with nervous energy. After everything that happened last night, I feel a little scattered, like dandelion puffs on a strong wind. Where will I go? Where will I land?

I know right now I have one singular destination: the bar where I left my car last night, along with my purity and my long-held solitude. Even though it's a glorious, clear Saturday afternoon, my mind is clouding over with worry and regret. I do not regret what transpired between my handsome stranger and me last night. I know it was a long time coming, and I can't pretend like it wasn't one of the single-most awe-inspiring nights of my life thus far. Learning that I, too, bear the capacity for darkness, but that there can truly be pleasure in the shadows if you venture there with the right companion. It feels strangely liberating in a way, even if my fear has not been completely vanquished. It still clings to the edge of my mind, pricking me like a needle every now and again, just so that I will not completely forget the dark place I come from.

I glance over at the driver again. He's another startlingly good-looking guy, with a serious expression that seems permanently hitched to his face. Dark eyes, dark hair, dark demeanor. I can completely understand how he might be an associate of the handsome but rough-edged stranger who changed my life irretrievably last night. They both share a sort of grim defiance that makes them slightly intimidating but also gives them this fire that is difficult to tear away from. I don't want to look away, but I know I must. Still, the silence settling into the space between us feels as heavy as a shroud, and I don't think I can withstand the whole ride to the bar this way. So finally, in a voice as soft and muted as a child's, I speak.

"Thank you again for driving me back," I murmur. "I don't know what got into me last night to make me leave my car behind. It's very... out of character for me."

"Oh, I have a pretty good idea of what—or who—got into you last night," the man called Breaker remarks pointedly.

I feel the rosy blush spread across my cheeks, my heart thumping like crazy. Does he know what happened? Does he know what I gave up last night? And much worse still: does he know who I am and why it even matters at all?

"Are you friends with him Do you know him well?" I ask, trying not to sound too eager.

I have a feeling my interest is impossible to miss, though. After all, I'm dying to know more about the mysterious, handsome stranger who swept into my barren world and injected hot, bright lightning into it. I want to know everything about him and commit it to memory. I don't know if I will ever see him again, but the experience he gave me should be enough to sustain me for a long time. Or so I hope. But there's this quiet, niggling worry in the back of my mind telling me that no matter how hard I try to resist it, to pull away and pretend like none of it has anything to do with me, I'll never get past it. I will never forget. And now that I have gotten a light taste of the kind of pleasure I've been denying myself all these years... how can I ever go back? I will always be craving more. I'm addicted after just one taste.

"You really want to know more about him?" Breaker says.

The man driving the car looks over at me with his dark eyes narrowed, his heavy brow knitted tightly in the middle. There's a half-smile playing around his lips, like he can't decide whether to be amused or disturbed by my questions. I wonder if I've danced too close to the fire. Maybe I have revealed too much of myself to this man already. What has come over me lately? I used to be oh so good at wrapping up all of my feelings and memories, tying them up with a pretty bow, and shoving them into some dusty, cobwebby corner to be forgotten about.

But I can't stop thinking about him. I can't seem to put him back in the box.

Breaker appears a little put-out by my lack of interest in him, and I get it. He's the kind of intriguing stranger most women are probably drawn to. He has a romantic type of bad-boy charm, but perhaps my very own mysterious man has inoculated me with immunity against Breaker's appeal.

His eyes drag back to focus on the dusty, empty country road in front of us.

"Yes. I don't even know his name. But he saved me from that awful guy in the bar. I-I just want to be able to properly thank him," I manage to get out.

"So you're not one of Diesel's girls, then," he muses aloud.

I frown and tilt my head to one side. "Diesel? What do you mean?" I ask.

He shakes his head and tightens his grip on the wheel so that his knuckles go white. "Don't you worry about that. If you don't belong to him already, count your blessings," he says.

"I don't go out very often. I don't think I would have crossed paths with someone named Diesel," I reply. Then I brighten up. "Unless Diesel is the name of the man who took me home last night."

Breaker snorts and rolls his eyes. "Hell, no. Trust me, you would have had a much different experience if it was Diesel who took you home. Especially because he probably would not have taken you to your home, if you know what I mean," he says.

I don't. I don't know what he means. But I'm not interested in that anyway. I just want to eke out as much information about my mystery guy as possible.

"Then tell me about him—the one who saved me last night. Please. At least let me know his name," I pleaded softly.

Breaker looks over at me with an almost pitying expression, which I hate. I cannot stand the feeling of being pitied. Few things make me feel so hopeless and childlike as pity. Sympathy, maybe. But pity? I would rather be met with anger or hatred than that.

"His name is Bones," Breaker reveals flatly.

"Bones?" I repeat, raising an eyebrow with incredulity. "That doesn't sound like a real name to me."

"Well, does Breaker sound like a real name to you?" he points out.

I shrug. "Okay. I see your point. But why can't I know his actual birth name? Is it a secret for some reason? Why? And what about you?" I ask, firing off question after question.

"You have a lot of questions bouncing around in that pretty little head of yours," Breaker growls. "You would do better to clamp down on some of them. There are things out here in the world you do not want the answer to. That may seem hard to believe, but—"

"No," I interrupt suddenly and fiercely. "It's not hard to believe. Trust me."

Breaker gave me a look that indicated he was starting to see another side to me. I know what he probably thought when he first saw me. I'm not a fool. I know what I look like in the predatory eyes of men. I know how dainty and wide-eyed and innocent I can appear to those who don't know me well. I know I seem breakable. Naive. Sheltered. And all of those things are true, but that's not all there is to know about me. I'm more complicated than any of them ever notice.

I look easy, but I'm not. I'm hard. They just haven't seen me tested yet.

"Here. You want to reach out to Bones so badly, I'll give you his phone number," Breaker says, surprising me.

I hastily whip out my simple burner phone to type in a new contact under the name BONES. He recites the number to me and I file it away, my heart racing. It's been so long since I programmed a new number into my collection. I change phones so often and I live such an isolated existence that there are rarely more than one or two saved contacts in my phone at any given time. And those are usually 9-1-1 and some food delivery company. To have a real phone number that connects with a man like Bones… it almost feels like too much power.

"Tell me about him. Please," I beg.

Breaker sighs, shaking his head. "Bones is… Bones. He's a good man, if that's what you're wondering. Rough around the edges, like the rest of us. He's seen some dark shit in his life, but it hasn't turned him completely dark. He deserves a good woman to keep him company," Breaker tells me emphatically.

I bite my lip, guilt rising like bile in my throat.

"And what if I'm not a good woman?" I murmur.

Breaker's face crumples into a bemused smile and he chuckles grimly. "I don't think a girl like you is capable of being bad," he remarks. "Don't worry; whatever you're afraid of, whatever you're hiding, Bones has seen worse."

I know he probably means all of this in a helpful way, but it doesn't work for me. Instead, I just feel slighted. Overlooked. Dismissed. Like all the nightmares I have suffered through mean nothing at all to this world-hardened man gripping the steering wheel. Like Bones would scoff at the demons that have been trailing after and haunting me all these long, lonely years.

When we reach the bar, I listen to the crackle of the vehicle tires on gravel, my heart starting to pound harder and faster. I see my trusty little car parked in the back left corner of the lot, untouched and safe. I breathe a sigh of relief to see it there unharmed. Out in the country like this, you never know who or what might mess with your stuff. Especially a solid, dependable vehicle. There are some who would kill for what I have, and I know it.

Breaker cuts the engine and hops out to come around and open the side door before I even have a chance to pop my seatbelt open. He offers me a hand and I take it, letting him help me down to my feet. I rub my shoulders, shivering slightly in the brisk air. It's sunny, at least, but still chilly. I look across to my car longingly, then back at the bar. I remember now that the bartender must have taken my keys, which means I have to follow along as Breaker strolls into the bar. My whole body is on high alert as I step through the doors, my eyes scanning the room for any hint of danger. And, of course, for any sign of Bones.

Breaker abandons me pretty much the second he walks into the bar, and for a moment I'm a little hurt, until I see him walk right up to a pretty girl smiling at him from the bar counter. He gives her an equally adoring smile and envelops her in his strong arms, and I can tell immediately that there must be a lot of real, true love between them. I can feel the tension and fear held in my body starting to loosen up and melt away as I watch the pair of them softly murmur to each other in the way lovers do. Or at least, the way I assume lovers do. I don't exactly have a wealth of positive experiences with "love" to reflect on. But they seem happy, and that makes me feel less afraid of being in the bar where the fight broke out. Besides, it's daytime now and the ambiance here is a far cry from the grim grittiness of last night. I decide to be brave and strut right up to the counter, though I can't resist my nervous habit of twirling a lock of hair around my finger as I slide onto a barstool and wave to get the bartender's attention.

He gives me a nod and comes sauntering over, swinging my car keys around his pointer finger. He gently sets it down on the glossy counter in front of me, bracing himself on his elbow.

I give him a smile. "Thank you so much for holding onto my keys. I feel like I need to apologize again for things getting... out of hand last night," I say softly.

He shrugs. "Don't mention it. Happens all the time here, girly. And it wasn't your fault. That guy had it comin'. I saw what he tried to do to you," he says gruffly.

I blink in confusion. "So it's not just in my head? He really did try to... to roofie me?"

The bartender nods slowly, his eyes looking around the bar as though searching for any signs of trouble. "I'm sure it's not the bastard's first time doing it either," he grumbles.

"Really? Do you know him? What's his name? Who is he?" I fire off quickly.

"Slow down, girly. Don't get ahead of yourself," the bartender says. "Look, the guy's name is Brandon. Local jarhead with a rich daddy. He's a scumbag. I wish somebody would bring him down to size."

I feel my face flush at that idea. I shake my head vigorously.

"Not me. I don't want to cause any trouble," I insist. I lower my voice and lean in closer. "In fact, if you could just keep this quiet, I'd appreciate it. I don't plan on pressing charges and I kind of just want to forget it ever happened. Actually, forget I was ever here to begin with."

A look of profound sadness crosses over the bartender's face for just a flicker of an instant, and I feel that familiar pull in my gut. Pity. More pity. I can't bear it.

But he sighs, "You got it, girly. You were never here and it never happened. But listen—be careful out there, alright? You got lucky last night, but it could've gone worse."

"I know. Trust me, I know," I reply heavily.

I slide off my barstool and walk out of the bar, clutching my keys. My shoes crunch on the gravel as I walk to my car, already pulling up my phone contacts list so I can potentially reach out to Bones. My heart races like mad. I don't even know what to say to him. There are so many feelings I want to express, but I don't know how to convert them into words. And the last thing I need is to come off like a blubbering, hysterical mess of a person in his eyes. I want him to think of me as a smart, put-together, sexy young woman. Not some terrified ingénue who can't hold her own. Maybe that's the truth, but it's not the reality I want anymore.

But just as I'm about to dial his number, a push notification appears on my screen, interrupting me. For a split second I just groan and move to instinctively delete the notification, until my eyes land on the name in the headline and my blood runs cold.

"Jailed Pedophile Murray Smyth Awaits Appeal Hearing for Compassionate Release."

Murray Smyth. Three syllables which have echoed in my head and left a foul taste on my tongue ever since I was twelve years old. Angrily, I hit the button to dismiss the notification and pause to draw in a slow, deep breath as I climb behind the wheel of my car. I lock the doors. Once, twice, three times in a row. I put on my seatbelt. I turn and look into the backseat, scanning it for signs of break-in. Bile rises in my throat and I swallow it back down, feeling like there are fish swimming around in my nervous belly. Then, the trembles start. My fingers first, then passing through the rest of my body until I'm shaking all over. With tears starting to blur my vision, I toss my phone down into the passenger seat and lean forward to gently rest my forehead on the steering wheel.

I murmur to myself, "It's okay. You're safe. Nobody knows where you are. Nobody knows what you've been doing. Nobody knows your name. They can't track you down—not here. He's far away, doing time. They won't let him out. They would never. You just have to be more careful, just in case."

I heave a deep breath and open my eyes again. Sufficiently pepped-up, I nod to myself as I turn the keys in the ignition and the engine rumbles to life. I slowly and cautiously pull through the parking lot and pause, looking both ways before I can drive out onto the main road. But something catches my eye and I do a double take.

A man on a motorcycle, his head blocked by a helmet except for his piercing gaze, which pulls away from the bar, over to land on me. He stares at me openly, which sends a shiver of horror down my back. He's watching me. I have to get out of here. I peel out in the opposite direction, and even though he doesn't make any indication to follow me, I can't help but watch my rearview mirror the whole way home.

BONES

I glare at the flickering screen in front of me, where the live security camera feed is showing me everything that just happened upstairs. I can't hear any of it, of course, but I've been glued to the screen since Lauren walked in, and I stare at the door thoughtfully for a minute or so after she leaves.

Breaker wanted me down here while Lauren arrived. I'm not happy about it. I should have been up there talking to her and making sure she isn't still in any danger, but Breaker insisted that I stay out of sight. He wanted to see if she'd act differently with me not around.

But I'm starting to lose patience for all that careful nonsense. Being overly cautious isn't what saved Lauren last night, and it's not what I feel good doing right now down here when I could be up there checking up on her myself. I'm the one who started all this, and I want to be the one who sees it through.

Suddenly, my phone buzzes, and I look down to see that I have a text from an unfamiliar number. I furrow my brow as I open it and see a very different kind of text on the screen than I usually get.

Got your number from Breaker. Don't be a stranger.

At the end of the second sentence is the emoji of a lipstick imprint, and when I first read it, I can't keep a smile off my face. The thought of taking her phone and getting her number while she was sleeping had crossed my mind, but even I didn't want to be that invasive at the time. But the bubbly feeling in my chest only lasts a minute as I re-read the first part of that text, and my brow furrows.

I shut the laptop and storm out of the office, through the clubhouse bar and upstairs to where the guys have already resumed business as usual in the bar. Big Daddy and Skid are shooting pool, and Breaker is talking to Kate at the far end of the bar before he sees me, kisses her, and starts coming my way.

But then he sees the look on my face, and he realizes he's about to deal with a situation.

"Who the hell said you could give her my number, Prez?" I demand, stepping forward to confront the prez without fear.

He's surprised by my outburst and strides

forward to meet me, but the rest of the bar only gives us a passing glance. It isn't all that uncommon for any two of us to have a shouting match with one another, sometimes with even more people involved. That's just how we talked. Hell, it was how we blew off steam so that we didn't blow each other's heads off sometimes.

"'Scuse me, Bones?" he says, crossing his arms and standing his ground as I march up to him with a hard glare.

"What happened to her being a liability?" I bark, throwing my hands up. "You could have just given my real-ass number to one of Diesel's people!"

"Brother, I did you a *favor*," Breaker says, brow knit.

I want to retort that I should just start handing out Breaker's number to groupies, but I know that's a line too far to cross. I don't want to compare Lauren to some thirsty groupie, and the look in Breaker's eye makes me suspect he knows that.

"So what," I say, "one ride with her and suddenly you're sure she's trustworthy? What'd she say to you, huh?"

"Not a whole lot," Breaker snapped back, raising his voice to match mine. "And what she did have to say was mostly about you!"

"I-" I stop. That legitimately takes me by surprise, and I don't know what to say for just long enough for a smug smile to spread across Breaker's face before he continues.

"Brother, I know where you're coming from, I really do, but if she were in Diesel's pocket," he says, "don't you think she'd have been more interested in the MC's leader than you?"

"You don't know-" I say, stopping myself short, but it's hard to push through his logic. "That girl is a hell of a lot sharper than she lets on, Prez. Don't let her fool you into thinking any different."

"She wasn't trying to fool me about anything, except maybe how interested she is in you," he chuckled, and both of our shoulders slowly relaxed as the tension between us faded. "No, I hear you, Bones—you've got trouble on your hands, but it ain't the kind of trouble Diesel has his hand in."

Breaker turns and starts to make his way back to the bar, but I scoff before begrudgingly step up to it further down as Eli starts pouring me a shot of whiskey preemptively.

"Fine, maybe she's not a spy. But even if you're right," I growl, "I don't need to get tangled up with some high-maintenance girl when we've got plenty of our own shit to handle. You shouldn't have given her my number without asking."

"Wasn't like you were about to storm out of there and give it to her yourself," Breaker says, raising his beer to him and tipping it toward me. "Besides," he adds, wrapping an arm around Kate who's raising an eyebrow at me, "women make the world go 'round, brother."

I stare at the two of them for a moment as Breaker turns to kiss Kate on the lips, and I roll my eyes, shaking my head and wondering what kind of a fit Breaker would have thrown if I had tracked down Kate and brought her here back before they got together. But I suppose he has a point. I watched Lauren every second that she was in the bar from the cameras downstairs, and I was no psychologist, but I could read body language. She wasn't interested in anyone in the bar, least of all Breaker.

My jealousy isn't just annoying because it's unfounded, it's annoying because I don't even like feeling jealous over her. But goddamn, I cannot get her out of my head.

Just as I toss back the whiskey in a vain hope that it'll take the edge off this day, the door of the bar swings open, and Ironside's dripping form storms in, not even bothering to take his jacket off as he looks around at everyone whose attention just snapped to him.

"We need to ride," his gravelly voice said with the kind of severity we all knew better than to blow off. "Our man in the police force just reported that Mayor Harley made an emergency call to the station."

"On a Sunday?" I say, sliding my empty shot glass away and furrowing my brow.

"Exactly," he says with a nod to me."

"We need to go have a word with him," Breaker says, standing up. "This can't be a coincidence. Nothing happens in Pine Haven, and something like last night might be just enough to get people excited. Let's go."

Minutes later, we're on our bikes and blazing down the road in the rain, carving a clear path through town with our ride as we storm into the nice part of town where the mayor's house is. Like most local politicians, the mayor of Pine Haven belongs to a wealthy family that goes back a long ways, and even in a small town, his neighborhood is the one with the biggest houses, the most manicured lawns, and the fanciest cars.

When our handful of rugged, kutte-wearing outlaws rolls in on our thundering bikes, we draw some attention. The first few times we visited the mayor, someone called the cops on us. But by now, we have made perfectly clear that we're the ones who'll do what needs to be done to keep life in Pine Haven happy, even if that means sidling up to the mayor's house and having a friendly chat every now and then.

As we pull up to the large, three-story house that looks big enough to house a dozen or so people at least, a white-faced gentleman peers down at us with fear in his eyes from a ground-floor window. I grin at him as he vanishes from sight, and a moment later, Mayor Hartley opens the door with a tight, mirthless smile as he waves to us. We dismount and stride up to the door, Breaker and I in front, Ironsides and Big Daddy taking up the rear while the two younger members who joined us hang back and watch the bikes. It helps to maintain a presence if we have people outside, too.

Discourages nosy neighbors, to boot.

"Bob," Breaker greets the mayor as we make our way inside uninvited. "Good to see you again. Enjoying the weather today? Perfect for a ride."

"I'll have to take your word for it," Mayor Hartley says as my dirty boots stomp across a pristine white carpet.

The interior of the guy's house is a joke. At a glance, it looks like a generically classy semi-rich guy's house, with high ceilings and a fancy chandelier in the living room and a fireplace loaded with pictures of him and his associates over the years, usually shaking hands. These are dotted with other pictures of him hunting with his friends, and a few family pictures are scattered around the rest of the house, along with a peculiar maritime aesthetic. The guy likes his ships in bottles, and even has what looks like a ship's steering wheel mounted on the wall like a deer trophy.

"Where do you think he hunted that one?" Big Daddy whispers to Ironsides behind me, pointing up to the ship wheel, and I snort a laugh.

As they mayor shuts the door behind us, he looks us all up and down with an uneasy face. "I want to say I wasn't expecting you all today, but I suppose that would be a lie."

"We'd love to give you more heads up, if you'd just do me the courtesy of letting us know when we need to talk ahead of time," I say as I 'admire' some of the decor.

"Why don't you tell us what's on your mind, Mr. Mayor?" Breaker asks, flopping down on the elegant couch and putting his boots up on the glossy mahogany coffee table. "Oh, excuse me," he says, and he shifts his legs so that his boots are resting on a marble coaster.

Breaker doesn't want to explicitly mention that we have a man in the police force watching him. The mayor probably either knows or has a strong suspicion, but if he hears it from Breaker, it would be impossible to justify not doing a clean sweep of the force and rooting out our informant who keeps us up to date on a lot of what goes on in Crooks County.

The mayor rubs his forehead and holds back a sigh, stepping over to a large armchair across the room to sit down. He probably wants to feel like he has some semblance of control here, and as tempting as it is to mess with the pompous ass, we do need his cooperation—coerced or otherwise.

"If there's no sense in at least offering you a

drink," he murmurs before speaking up. "Look, you didn't give me any choice. Last night, one of your people started a bar fight with a man named Brandon Robinson. That's *Master Sergeant* Brandon Robinson of the US Marines," he adds meaningfully, making eye contact with each and every one of us.

I can't help but feel a jolt of pride at this new info about the wannabe rapist. I knew the guy I took down was military, but damn. Breaker doesn't look quite as happy about that news, though.

"The man isn't just a war hero in the eyes of the people of Pine Haven," Mayor Hartley goes on. "He happens to be the son of a congressman. I know I can't exactly put signs on people to tell you who not to bother, but good god, couldn't you have shown some discretion?"

"Your 'war hero' didn't show any discretion when he tried to slip that roofie into that girl's drink!" Breaker says before I can stop him.

The mayor's eyes widen, and he looks to me for confirmation. I look pissed that Breaker just outed me as the one who got into a fight with this 'Master Sergeant', but I'm even more pissed that he's saying it at all.

"We don't just pick fights," Breaker goes on. "That might be some bikers, but it's not the Heartbreakers, and I stand by him on this. Your congressman's boy was trying to date rape a friend of the club's, and we have multiple witnesses who'll swear to it."

"Good Christ," the mayor says, letting his face fall into his hands before he massages his temples and clenches his eyes.

"Breaker," I say, even more pointedly, "she *also* said pretty goddamn clearly that she didn't want to press charges, if I heard you right."

"It doesn't matter," the mayor says, looking disgusted but weary. "He's a well-respected man with his whole life ahead of him, this kind of scandal can't get out."

"Hey, no, bullshit on that too!" I snap. "That piece of shit was just going to get away with that if I hadn't stepped in. Mayor Hartley, are you going to tell me a woman's life is worth less than some snotty rich kid's reputation?"

"And his father's," the mayor says, opening his eyes and glaring at me.

That pisses me off so much that I take a step forward, fully intending to show the mayor exactly what I thought about that sentiment, but I feel a steel hand grab my belt and hold me back. It's Ironsides, and he gives me a glare that urges me to stay put. I'm not cowed by any of the men in this room, and I'm getting more agitated by the second, but Ironsides gives me just enough time to think twice about what I was about to do.

"Gentlemen," the mayor says, "I understand there seems to be a lot of personal baggage here, but the facts are that word got out about what you did last night, regardless of circumstances," he says, looking up at me. "And because of what you did, I spent the morning on the phone with that Marine's father, who's now threatening to pull funding for a town development project that will keep a *lot* of hardworking Americans in their jobs."

In the brief pause that follows, the mayor finds his spine and presses ahead.

"The congressman has warned me that unless I put *you*, apparently, in the county jail on aggravated assault charges, that money and those jobs go away. And if I let it get out that a congressman's son was doing something like that—if it truly happened— then the consequences could be even worse. My hands are tied, and frankly, I don't know what the hell you people want me to do about that," he finished, leaning forward and speaking through nearly gritted teeth.

"Mayor Hartley," Breaker says, standing up slowly and putting a hand out between us, "let me handle this. This is all fresh right now. Bones is one of my men, and I'll deal with him."

"Thank you," the mayor says, sighing. "I don't expect to hear the last of this, just, please, touch base with me before acting rashly."

We left the house moments later in silence, but once we reach the bikes, Breaker stops and rounds on me with a red face.

"What the fuck was that in there, Bones?" he growls, stepping toward me.

"That was me respecting Lauren's wishes," I fire back, holding my ground feeling my blood boil. "Unlike you."

"What was that?" he says, getting closer. "Because all I heard in there was you making us look divided in front of someone we need to have a healthy fear of us."

"And I heard you talking like a politician!" I snap. "What was that 'let me handle it' mafia bullshit? And you know what? I don't appreciate the hint that *I* should be apologizing for something I'd do again, if I had the chance!"

"What you did was make a scene that could turn the town against us!" Breaker shouted.

"Because nobody else had the backbone to!" I retort.

Breaker and I glare at each other while the others watch silently.

"You need to blow off some steam," Breaker finally growls through clenched teeth, pointing down the road. "Go for a ride, Bones. Alone. Meet us back at the clubhouse when you're ready to get your act together."

I glare at him for another few moments, but if I stay any longer, I'll start swinging. Without giving him the satisfaction of hearing me curse under my breath, I storm to my bike and peel away from the sidewalk, leaving a nice black streak in front of the mayor's house.

Through the rain, it doesn't take me long to steer my bike to the one place I know I can rein myself in the way I need to and get my head clear.

I ride toward Lauren's house.

LAUREN

I sit with my legs curled up underneath me on the sofa, flipping uselessly through the channels on my tiny second-hand television set. I picked it up at a yard sale years ago, when I first moved to the area. I'm not a girl with a lot of money to spend. I have to make it go a long way, and if that means sifting through people's junk while an old woman watches me with hawk eyes and continually tries to recruit me for her church, then so be it. I have managed to amass most of my furnishings and decor from similarly downtrodden origins. My sofa is from a thrift store sale. My kitchen appliances were bought on auction, second-hand. My clothes come from thrift shops, too, even most of my shoes. If there is one upside to living this frugal, isolated lifestyle, it must be that I can at least claim a pretty sharply reduced biological footprint on the earth. In fact, I have gotten so accustomed to hiding that I hardly make much of an impression in the world in general. Few people know me. Even fewer know where I come from, who I used to belong to. What horrible last name used to follow my first name. I kept the first: Lauren. It's not for his sake, but for mine. It is the only piece of proof defining who I used to be that I have carried with me all this time. It's the only thing that truly belongs to me. And when the same evil, diabolical devil of a man has deliberately robbed me of every other little thing I used to have, a name becomes more important than you could ever know.

"Looks like the rural community around Pine Haven is going to be wet, wet, wet for the next day or so, with large storm clouds moving in over the area. Expect heavy rains and thunderstorms until tomorrow mid-morning, when it's projected to start clearing up. Folks, there's no better time than today to curl up with a good book or a loved one and ride out the inclement weather," announces the weather guy on the TV in front of me.

I smile softly to myself, even though I change the channel. I glance out the window, listening to the soothing tap-tap of rain pattering against the glass pane behind the lacy curtains. I have always been a fan of stormy weather. Maybe it's just because I already spend almost all of my time cooped up here, rain or sunshine, and it feels less egregious to do so when the weather would keep me trapped inside anyway. It's the perfect excuse to do what I always do: lock all the doors and windows and be alone.

Sure, I get lonely. Who doesn't? It's human nature to want to reach out, to connect. But I've seen too much. I've stood much too close to the flames to be drawn out by fire. I much prefer the rain. It feels safer. Like I'm swaddled up in a cozy, slightly dreary cocoon.

And tonight I definitely need extra comfort, because in my hand right now is my burner phone, with the name MURRAY SMYTH plastered across the top of the screen. I can't seem to stop reading article after article about the major appeal coming up in his case. No matter how horrified it makes me feel, how far down into the depths of my wildest fears it manages to reach, I can't stay away. I have to know what is happening. I have to be prepared. Judging from the way the article is worded, the author doesn't appear to think Smyth will be granted his appeal for compassionate release. After all, he's not ancient. He's only in his fifties. Only twice my age. And he's only been in jail for thirteen years, nowhere near as long as the bastard deserves. If it were up to me, he would never be released. Hell, if it were up to me, he wouldn't exist anymore. I am so tired of sharing this planet with him. If I never see or hear of him again, I'll be satisfied. But the world can't stop pointing to him, drawing his image out of the dark. It feels like I've buried his body somewhere in the far-back recesses of my mind, and these articles just dig him right back up and breathe life into his filthy body.

Sometimes, when it gets to be almost too much to bear, I imagine him dead. Those hands falling limp so they can no longer touch. Those eyes going dark so they can no longer watch. It's the only way I'll ever be safe from him, and I know it. But the state is lenient. As far as they know, he's only offended once. Granted, it was an absolutely monumental offense, and I think it should be more than enough to put him away forever. But the parole board is gentle. They have mercy for the man with the entrancing eyes and the winning smile.

I hate that I can see traces of those eyes and that smile in the mirror. Like he's imprinted himself on me somehow. Our blueprints overlapping and clashing together.

Suddenly, cutting through the fog of anxiety and clattering rain, I hear another familiar sound that makes the hairs on the back of my neck stand up. A motorcycle engine revving. Getting louder and louder by the moment.

And closer, too.

"Shit," I murmur as I drop my phone and switch off the TV.

Keeping low to the ground, I pull out the baseball bat from underneath my thrifted coffee table and wield it in both hands as I creep slowly to the door. My heart is pounding. Adrenaline pulses through my veins. I stand up ever so slightly to peer out the nearby window and, to my surprise, I actually recognize the face of the man on the motorcycle.

It's Bones. I would recognize his face anywhere. It's forever seared into my mind.

I relax for a moment, acknowledging that at least it's probably not the same guy who was watching me outside of the bar yesterday. But then I tense up again as it dawns on me that even though I have his number, I never actually reached out to Bones at all. And after he went away, I have started to have second thoughts about the dark pleasure he helped me explore. That is a side of myself I've kept hidden for so long, and for good reason. It felt good to let go and give in to my desires for once, but I worry it's too dangerous. After all, I've spent so long trying to cage in that wild beast that lurks deep inside of me, scratching to burst free at the slightest inclination. All my hard work will go to waste if I let a man like Bones break me. I can't allow him to see the truth of who I am. Where I hail from. It's an indelible scar on my soul, one that will someday lay me bare before my maker and cause me to lose paradise. I know it. A girl like me can't come from a place like that and make it to heaven in the end. My dark destiny was written in the stars long before I was even born.

But then, still clutching my baseball bat like a

lifeline, I watch surreptitiously from the window as Bones rolls to stop. He cuts the engine of his motorbike and rakes his fingers back through his hair. I am immediately smacked in the face with the sense memory of those same glorious fingers combing through my hair. Tangling in it. Pulling my hair to guide me as I sucked and choked on his cock. I can feel my body warming up and opening to him at just the mere thought of it. He looks devilishly sexy as he dismounts the bike, those long, powerful legs in boot cut dark jeans. He's wearing a plain white t-shirt with a black leather jacket over it. Fingerless gloves to protect his hands from the rain and wind while still allowing him dexterity. He shakes his hair out, drops of rainwater flying everywhere as the storm clouds crackle and loom overhead. He's dripping wet from head to toe, but he manages to look gorgeous despite it. And when he starts sauntering up the front walkway to my door, I feel like I might pass out, my heart is hammering away so hard. He raises a fist to knock at the door.

Thump-thump-thump. Heavy and sharp.

I pause for a moment, toying with the idea of just pretending not to be home. It's easier than facing up to him. But then I remember that my car is parked outside. It's obvious that I'm here right now. So, with a deep breath of trepidation, I disengage all four locks on the door and pull it open just a crack to reveal his face, slick with rain and frowning at me.

He looks mad. There's a pulsating, angry energy to him I can't ignore, and it makes me feel flimsy and wispy by comparison to him.

"Bones," I murmur by way of a greeting.

"Lauren," he growls back. "Are you going to let me in or not?"

I swallow hard. I know I should turn away. I should slam the door shut and bolt all the locks. But it's raining outside and he's wet and he's looking at me with those luminous, powerful eyes… so I open the door farther, letting him push into the house. He immediately sheds his damp jacket, draping it on the coat rack by the door.

"You came back," I mumble softly.

He rounds on me with those eyes flashing. "I had to," he replies.

"And you seem angry about something," I point out.

"I am," he snarls, backing me farther into the foyer. I look up at him with round eyes.

"Why? What did I do?" I ask meekly.

"You're just going to let that asshole Brandon try and assault you? You told the bartender you don't want to even press charges?" he hisses. "He deserves to be punished for what he did."

"No. No, I can't," I protest, shaking my head.

"You have to. You can't let this go, Lauren," he insists.

"No!" I say, louder this time. "I know who he is

now. I know how powerful he is. His father is well-known and respected. Whatever he says, goes. Nobody will ever believe me. They won't believe you either, Bones. You've got to get out of town before this bows up any bigger than it already is. We can't face him. He's got connections."

"I don't give a damn who he is or who his father is!" Bones growls. "He tried to assault you. He fucked with your drink. I saw it happen."

"Don't you understand? It doesn't matter what the truth is," I whisper as tears start to burn annoyingly in my eyes. "All that matters is the story, and his story will be stronger than yours or mine. I can't let you go down for this, Bones. You saved my life. Please, listen to me: you have to get the hell out of dodge."

"That's not how I operate," he shoots back gruffly.

I slump back against the wall, letting the tears roll down my cheeks. I know how hysterical I must look. How weak. But he doesn't get it. He could never understand.

"It's all happening again," I sniffle. "I'm cursed. That's what it is. A curse. I keep trying to run away. I keep trying to hide. But that darkness will always follow me. It always catches up, no matter how far I go. I'm a jinx, Bones. I'm bad luck. I've been bad ever since I was conceived. You can't get tangled up with me. I'll ruin your life."

"What the hell are you talking about?" Bones demands, though I detect a note of sympathy in his voice. But not pity. At least it's not pity.

"You'd never understand. Just… believe me. I'm cursed, okay? I break everything I touch. It's in my damn blood," I sob.

Bones softens a little and reaches for me, to pull me into a tight hug. But as much as I want to give in, to let his warm embrace soothe the fear away for however long we can keep it at bay, I know it's better if I make as clean a break as possible. He's already rescued me once. I can't make him do it again. So I push him away, recoiling from his touch. I shake my head, backing away and then turning to go up the stairs. To my horror, he follows me. I can feel and hear his heavy footsteps behind me. Why won't he leave? Why doesn't he get it?

"Leave me alone! I'm trying to help you!" I shout back at him over my shoulder.

"Come back. It'll be okay, I promise," he tries to soothe me.

"You don't understand!" I protest, taking the stairs two at a time.

"I understand a lot more than you think I do," Bones says cryptically. "I found the clipping, Lauren. I found the article. I know."

My whole body freezes up and I slowly pivot around to look at him. Even though he's a few stairs lower than me, he's still taller than I am. I can scarcely breathe, much less speak.

But I manage to croak out, "What?"

His eyes lock with mine as he says emphatically, "I know about the kidnapping."

"The kidnapping?" I repeat in a flat, dead tone.

He nods. "Yes, Lauren. I know you were kidnapped by a very, very bad man."

My shoulders slump and tears prickle in my eyes. I shake my head. "No. You don't understand. You've got the story all wrong. Don't even try to understand, alright? Just leave me alone! Please!" I whisper bitterly.

Bones reaches to take my wrist but I manage to pull away and dart up the rest of the stairs. He's hot on my trail as I fling open my bedroom door and dive inside, slamming it shut behind me. Just as his hand starts to turn the knob, I engage the double lock, and he can't get in. He tries the door a few more times.

"Come on, little girl. Open up. I'm here to help you," he insists.

"No. Go away," I sniff, wiping at my eyes.

There's a silence. A few moments turns into a minute. A few minutes. I hear his footsteps dissipating down the hall and I throw myself down into my bed, burying my face in my pillow. My whole body is wracked with sobs. I'm alone again. Just me and my past, facing up in the arena once again. I'll never be free of it. That darkness will follow me until my dying breath.

I'm so exhausted and stressed out that I start to doze a little, assuming that Bones has let himself out of the house and gone home. But a couple hours later, my eyelids flutter open and I look at the big bay window. It's after sunset. The sky is still stormy, but much darker than before. And then something else hits me—the smell of something delicious cooking. It's a strangely comforting fragrance. Butter and potatoes. Herbs. Sizzling meat.

My stomach growls plaintively and I sit up in bed, trying to figure out where the delicious smell could be coming from. I don't do a lot of cooking, myself, and the nearest neighbor is way too far off for me to ever smell their cooking. It dawns on me that someone must be here. In my house. My kitchen, to be more precise.

I gasp and rush across the room, unlocking and opening my door quietly. I stand there frozen in place for a moment, listening. I can hear the faint scrape of pots and pans downstairs, and the scent of cooking is much stronger now. My mouth waters and I realize I can't resist any longer. I quietly pad down the stairs and around the corner into the kitchen, my eyes widening at the sight of Bones dutifully cooking up some of the food I've had in my fridge and freezer all week. There are fluffy golden potatoes whipped with rosemary and butter. There are two steaks seasoned with black pepper and sea salt, sizzling in my one and only cast-iron skillet. Bones is holding a spatula in one hand, a steak knife in the other. Even though the sight of a mostly-strange man in my kitchen wielding a knife does frighten me, the softness in his eyes is enough to placate me for the time being.

Well, that and the tempting smell of a home-cooked meal.

"You look like you haven't been eating well," Bones says.

I hang my head, blushing. "I guess I've been too anxious to eat."

"You shouldn't skip meals," he chides me gently. "Sit down. It's ready."

I obediently take a seat at the quaint, two-seater table I picked up at a rummage sale at some back-woods church months ago. Bones brings over two plates heaped high with juicy, medium-rare steak and piles of whipped potatoes. I can hardly hold myself back at all. I hungrily rip into the meal while Bones watches me quietly. I can tell he's contemplating something. I still don't know why he's being so kind to me, but I can't deny how good the food is.

"I'm sorry I yelled at you and locked you out earlier," I tell him softly.

He shrugs. "I understand. You were afraid."

"You can't possibly understand," I sigh, setting

down my fork and knife. "But that's not your fault. I haven't given you a fair chance to understand."

"Okay. Try me," he says.

I take a deep breath, dread leaking in at the edges of my resolve. "You said you saw the clipping. The one about Murray Smyth," I begin, hating the way his name feels in my mouth. "And you assumed I was the girl he held hostage. I can see why you might think that. But that's not the truth."

Bones leans in closer, his brow furrowed. "Then tell me: what is the truth?"

Biting my lip, I admit the one thing I have been hiding all these years.

"The truth is…" I sigh, "I am Murray Smyth's daughter. I'm the one who turned him in."

BONES

*L*auren's confession hits me like a sack of bricks, and I can only just stare at her in disbelief. My jaw doesn't go slack, I don't go pale, and I don't break down worrying and fretting over her. I just meet her gaze and feel the weight of the words as she spills them. Goddamn, I've never thought of myself as an empathetic person, but something about the hollow look in her eyes when she says it tells me she's being honest. There could be no mistaking that.

"I saw 'Lockett' on an envelope addressed to you when I was looking for aspirin the other night," I say slowly, and her eyes widen as she realizes how I saw the article clipping.

"And that is my name," she says with a surprising sureness, as if she has rehearsed that in her head more than once. "The name I chose. Could you live with a name with that kind of baggage?"

I crack a smile. "You're talking to a guy named Bones, kid." The smile fades as I continue. "But you're right. Nobody would want to live with a name like that, by the sounds of things. But how does a girl your age...I mean, damn, I knew you were special, but how does a child figure all that out about her father?"

She opens and closes her mouth a few times as she stares at the food I have a feeling is going to go cold. She looks like she has asked herself the same question a dozen times, but the edge of desperation in her voice makes me realize that she might well have never told anyone about this. She's been so cagey about her past, but now that she's gotten the first of it blurted out, maybe the rest will come.

"Hey, I know I'm no therapist," I say, reaching under the table and taking her hand gently. It's so cold, but she curls it into a fist in my bigger hand and seems comforted by it. "I'm just an outlaw who knows a hurting soul when he sees one. Nobody's listening to us out here."

She nods softly in acknowledgement, and even though it doesn't look like much, I know she's listening to me. I know the look on a face like that. She's hard to reach, but she's in there.

"It was his shed," she says at last before swallowing hard. "I was the same age as her. It was just the two of us, and he never let me go into the shed. He said it was off-limits. There were dangerous things in there. Rats and bats that would eat me, is what he told me when I was really little. You know, the usual stuff they tell you when you're a kid. Things that are scarier than the reality."

She pauses when she says that, and she grimaces.

"Scarier than reality is supposed to be," she corrects herself, rubbing her eyes. "By the time I was twelve I...I had kind of figured out there weren't really rats in the shed. I assumed he just didn't want me poking around rusty tools or something. I was pretty well behaved back then. Most kids would have been driven crazy with curiosity, but I never had a reason not to trust him before then. I mean, I might have seen the signs if I had been looking for them." She looks bitter, and one of her fingers scrapes along the length of her fork idly. "...I think I didn't see the signs because of him."

"You think he was taking steps to hide things from you? That would make sense," I say, nodding. "People like that are careful. Very careful."

"Not just that," she says, barely above a whisper, and she shakes her head faintly before going on. "His birthday was coming up. I had overheard him mentioning wanting to get a plaque for his base-ment. I don't know what it was for, I just figured, a little wood and glue, how hard could it be? I wanted to surprise him. So I went in."

I watch her relive the moment with simple disbelief in her expression. The way she speaks and looks makes me think she has either kept this day out of her mind as much as she can, or she relives it every moment she's alone. It's hard to say which.

"I kind of rummaged for a bit, but I didn't know what I was looking for," she says, shaking her head and closing her eyes as she put a napkin to her nose for a moment. "It didn't take that long to hear the crying."

My heart drops, and I can't keep the wince off my face.

"Everything is kind of a blur after I found the hatch hidden under the floorboards," she says, keeping her eyes shut to prevent tears from falling out of them. "I remember trying to explain what I found to the police. And you know, it never hit me on that day when it was all happening that Dad had any idea the girl was in there," she says, opening her eyes and looking at me with a heartbreaking smile.

"How could you have?" I ask, shaking my head and furrowing my brow. "You were a kid, Lauren. You can't blame yourself for that."

"My family didn't see it that way," she says with a scornful laugh. "My father was...he was the favorite, plain and simple. He had always been the one the family knew was a good man who would be the most successful out of everyone. I think they saw me as slowing him down, I'm not sure, but they definitely thought I had opened the floodgates on the wrong man."

"Wrong man?" I ask, crossing my arms.

"They just couldn't believe what they were seeing on the news and what the detectives told them over the next few weeks," she says. "They couldn't believe their prodigy was capable of that. I'm not even sure what all they thought. Maybe they thought it was all a misunderstanding, and that because I misled the cops, the media had blown it out of proportion and ruined his life. I don't know."

"Jesus," I breathe.

"They didn't want anything to do with me," she says, sniffing. "The detectives found three more bodies in the woods where he used to go hunting, but they couldn't link them to him, and they just couldn't believe it."

"Where did you go?" I ask.

"Oh, I stayed," she says, "but I emancipated myself when I was sixteen and went as far away as I could. Now I'm here."

To my surprise, she picks up her fork and starts eating her steak and potatoes as if we had never had the conversation. I stare at her blankly for a few moments before speaking again.

"You said something about another reason you didn't suspect your dad," I say, and she stops eating again. This time, she seems unsure about whether to go on.

"I told you I have a darkness in me," she says quietly.

"If you're trying to tell me some of your dad rubbed off on that sweet twelve year old little girl you were," I say, trying to be reassuring. "You'll have hard time convincing me."

"You don't know me," she says, and her eyes flit up to mine so softly I'd barely notice, yet so sharply it almost stings.

"And you don't know me," I say, leaning on the table and giving her a thoughtful stare as she resumes eating. "And sweetheart, I know darkness."

"Do you?" she asks with simple interest.

I hesitate for a moment. I don't talk about my history, because I'd rather leave it as history. But Lauren just got a lot off her chest, and I can already tell she's starting to punish herself for it in her head. She wants to withdraw and let her own memories eat her up, and she might just succeed, if I don't take a step forward.

"I'm from Southern Cali," I say at last, leaning back and cutting into my cold steak. "Not much to tell you about how I got started. Fell in with some other assholes who had a lot of anger and nowhere to put it. Mom couldn't afford me, Dad wasn't interested in me, so it just happened over time. I didn't wind up in the good schools, I got the ones people gave you *looks* for," I say, chuckling at the memories.

They aren't the fondest, but they made me who I am today.

"What'd you do?" she asks, sounding almost like she wants to try me, find out what I've really got up my sleeve.

"The usual," I say. "Hotwire a car here and there, rob some asshole who's out of town for the week, get into fights I had no business getting in—and winning, most of the time," I add, glancing down at an old scar on my forearm. "That was shaping up to be my life, until my crew decided to knock over a convenience store just outside town that a buddy of mine owned."

She raises an eyebrow.

"It was just some guy I knew from high school before I got sent to correctional," I say, waving a dismissive hand. "Wasn't like we were best buds or anything, he was just a decent guy whose family owned the place. It was all they had, I didn't want to see them lose that. But you don't just say that to your gang of half a dozen pissed-off teenagers looking for some quick cash."

"So it was let him get robbed or...?" she asks, tilting her head to the side.

"Or figure out something else," I say with a shrug. "I figured the easiest thing to do would be to warn him, so I did. Thought he'd pack up and leave, or close up shop and try to move it."

"Your friends found out, didn't they?" she says,

eating more slowly now as she gets more interested in what I'm saying.

"Nah," I say, setting my utensils down and chewing a tough piece of meat for a bit. "That would have been too easy. Instead, my buddy was waiting for us with a shotgun."

"Oh my god," she breathes.

"We weren't in that store twenty seconds before one of my other friends was bleeding out on the ground after taking a shot dead-on," I say, staring across the table at her. "We ran and scattered, and I knew it was only a matter of time before they figured out I was the one who'd tipped the place off. Sure enough, it wasn't even a full day before I got a text from a friend telling me there was a price on my head. So, I packed up and rode. Rode across half the damn country until I fell in with a club that felt alright."

"And that's where you met the people I saw?" she asks. "Breaker, and the other guys?"

"Yes and no," I say. "We were running with a guy named Buzz back then. Older biker. Knew his way around the state. But not long after I joined, found out they were getting into human trafficking, and none of us liked that."

She looks shocked, as if she hadn't even considered that bikers would be in on that kind of trade.

"So, Breaker killed someone who had it coming, which is how we usually open the negotiating table,"

I say, remembering that night years ago and the chaos that had followed. "And we all broke up again, and we fell back together here in Crooks County. And that's what I know about 'darkness', since you asked," I add. "Spent my whole life in it. Lost friends over it. Killed because of it. People like me, we don't get a choice. We deal with it. Just like you."

"It's not the same," she says, getting up and going to the window, but I get up and follow her, not willing to let her get away from this one.

"Isn't it?" I ask.

"It lives *in* me, Bones," she says, staring out the window as I stand behind her, ready to grab her if need be. "He's my flesh and blood. He was able to do all that to those girls while I lived right there with him. That monster helped make me, what does that make me?"

"You can't blame yourself, Lauren," I say, taking a step closer.

"Everyone else did," she says, grasping the counter, and I step forward and hug her from behind. She holds back a sob as I hold her against me, but soon, the tension in her back eases and she drags her nails over the backs of my hands where she holds them. "I...I just want to let go for once, you know?"

"You can," I say in a low tone.

"No, I meant like last night," she confesses in a voice barely above a whisper before she turns to face me in my arms. "That's what last night was about. That's...why I even went out in the first place. I didn't know what I was doing. Maybe I did, I just- I've had my guard up so long, and I wanted to see what it was like to let it down and see what I can really be like. To see if I'm really...bad."

The way that word sounds on her lips tells me it has been haunting her all her life. And it explains so much while making me wonder so much more about this strange, incredibly strong girl. I hug her close to me and speak into her ear through her hair.

"You're not a bad girl, Lauren," I say in my deep, gruff voice. "You're not even an okay one, you're incredible. You lived through more before age sixteen most people do in their whole lives, and you came out of that fire. And I know good when I see it," I growl, and I press a kiss to her lips.

She gasps, but sighs into it slowly before a sob comes to her throat again, and she pulls back, turning her head away. I don't stop her in the slightest.

"I'm ashamed of myself," she murmurs.

"For what?" I ask.

Her soft eyes turn to mine, and I can see that glimmer of excitement buried deep down past all those shadows she's been keeping up. She looks me up and down, biting her lip, and her cheeks burn bright before she can muster the words.

"I...I liked it when you were...hard on me," she

says. "When you took control like that. I wasn't expecting it, but…"

"Like this?" I growl without missing a beat, and I reach around to pinch her ass with one hand while running my hands through her hair and grasping it, pulling her hair back a touch just to kiss her on the neck.

I feel her laughing through the kiss, and I can't help but smile as the tension melts away in the room. At least, it fades to make way for a very different kind of tension—the kind I like much more.

"Yeah," she says with a playful light in her expression. "Yeah, like that."

She puts a hand on my chest, slowly curling her fingers in, and I loom over her, looking down at her with nothing but pure adoration as my heavy heart thumps harder against my muscled pecs. I swipe my tongue over my lips and squeeze her ass more aggressively this time as my cock hardens, and I pull her tight against me. She whimpers softly as I start grinding my hips against hers, almost humping her against the kitchen sink before I swing her around to the table, holding her over it and running my hands up and down her body.

"Are you sure you want this, Lauren?" I ask, running my hands slowly and possessively over her. "If you want to explore the darkness with me…I can do that, but I need to know you're ready."

"Do *you* want this?" she asks, looking up at me with excited yet almost terrified expectation. "After everything you know about me?"

I lower my head until our foreheads touch, and I speak in an almost ominous growl.

"I've wanted you from the moment I saw you, Lauren," I rumble. "And I've wanted to keep you for myself so much that it scares me."

I feel goosebumps on Lauren's arms as she whispers, "Good."

"If you're ever not okay with something I do," I say, idly squeezing her breasts to show her just how much I can possess her. "Say 'heartbreaker.' Magic word. Everything stops."

"Oh," she laughs softly, "is that what your friend's name stands for?"

"Biggest turnoff I can think of," I laugh, and both our cheeks are rosy before we kiss again.

And this time, I feel my own darkness welling up inside me as I bite down on the soft, innocent flesh on her neck and bend her back.

"Do you like it hard and fast, little girl?" Bones hisses into my ear. "Do you want me to fuck you senseless? Until you're out of your mind?"

A tingle of warm, delicious pleasure spreads down from that soft point, through my whole body. A shiver runs down my spine, tiny goosebumps rising up on my skin as Bones takes both sides of my face in his hands. He strokes my cheeks, his thumbs slipping down the gentle slope of my nose, down to press at my full, plush lips. His thumb pushes against my bottom lip and I slowly part my lips, allowing him to push inside. My tongue lathes around his thumb and he lets out a low, aggressive growl. I close my lips around his thumb and suck on it, reveling in the bliss of having part of him in my mouth. He presses against my cheek from the inside, giving me the sensation of stretching out. It's a strange aching feeling that borders on perverse pleasure, and I moan, my eyes slowly closing as I give in to the feeling. But then I feel his free hand slide around to cup the back of my head. His fingers tangle softly into my hair, wrapping locks of my dirty blonde locks around his digits to get a stronger grasp on me. I can feel the raw, barely-restrained sexual energy burning inside of him, emanating a frantic glow that is more infectious than any disease I can think of.

His desire is contagious and addictive. It hits me in delicious waves and I feel my pussy starting to get slick and wet between my legs even though he's barely touched me anywhere yet. Just this mysterious stranger's presence is enough to light a fire in my heart. My eyes flutter open again, my long lashes trembling as I meet Bones's deep, penetrating gaze. His eyes look dark and deep, like two pools at the back of a cavern, filled with all manner of shadow and darkness. A sharp zap of fear electrifies my body. My brain sends a parade of panic signals, but I just let it wash over me.

I said I wanted to embrace the shadows that lurk inside of me. That is exactly what I intend to do. And there's not a single shred of doubt in my mind that Bones can take me there.

I tilt my head back, leaning into his arms as he cradles me backward onto the table. As he moves me, his arms and my ass shove the utensils and plates out of the way. Forks and steak knives clatter to the floor in a jangling heap. I let out a soft gasp of surprise and Bones immediately grins, that fire building ever higher in his eyes. Bones pushes me down, pressing me into the kitchen table hard. He leans in and grazes his teeth across my vulnerable throat, dragging a jagged line as though he's trying to slit my throat with his teeth. I can scarcely remember to breathe, my lungs constricting with mingled fear and adrenaline as he begins to bite down on the soft, ticklish flesh of my neck. First gently, then harder. I groan and shudder as the ache gets deeper. Sharper. I wonder for a moment if he's going to break skin.

I tremble in his arms, almost recoiling from the sharp pull of teeth on my neck. But he's so much stronger than I am, and he holds me in place, giving me no opportunity to get away. I know I should be afraid. There's a soft voice in the back of my mind, warning me that I am in danger. Reminding me that I am small. I am soft. I am putty in his hands, malleable to his every whim and wish. For so many long years I have lived in fear of accommodating the dark desires that fester and grow inside of me. I've been afraid to reach out and touch it, for fear that one touch will be more than enough to destroy me, turn me as dark and evil as the blood from which I was given life. I don't want to be like him. I refuse to be like him. And yet, I find myself here, lying open and unrepentant across the boundary line between what is good and what is evil.

Maybe I am of both worlds. Maybe I am the crossroads.

Either way, I can deny Bones nothing. Whatever he desires of me, he can take. Still, I can't help but protest a little when he scrapes me back across the kitchen table, my sweater riding up so that my bare spine scratches on the wood grain. He deftly unzips and tears down my jeans, tossing them across the room to drape over the back of the sofa. Cool, humid air hits my bare legs and I can't help but shiver. I can feel every knot and whirl of the wooden table under me.

"I'm going to get a splinter," I murmur breathlessly.

Bones leans in and snarls close to my ear, "Pain is good. You'll learn that in no time."

Outside, the thunderstorm rages on. Lightning cracks across the darkened night sky, rain pattering heavy and hard against the windowpane. Even through the thick walls of my little rental house, I can smell the distinctive, musky scent of wet earth and clay. Rain slicking down rivets of mud through the dewy, swaying grass. Flowers opening and closing to suck in the life-giving water. The forest seemed to swell and crowd around the house like a protective shield. From any window, you could see lush greenness encroaching closely. Here in my little house away from everything, there is no one to save me. No one to stop me.

"Tell me what you want, little girl," Bones hisses. "Tell me."

I bite my lip, afraid to answer, to breathe the words in my mind.

He glares into my eyes expectantly, but I'm too stunned. I'm speechless. Bones growls with impatience and says, "Fine. Fuck it. I'm not waiting anymore."

With that, he reaches down and wrenches my legs apart, his fingertips greedily groping and pressing into my soft thighs. I inhale sharply and hook my knees around his waist, pulling him in close while he runs his hands up and down my thighs, teasing me as I get slicker and wetter. I'm already ready for him, and we've only just begun, but I'm still too coy to let it all show just yet. I have to maintain my composure. I can't give it all away at once.

But when he yanks me close and starts to grind his crotch against mine, it's all I can do to keep from crying out and moaning with need. He gives me a devilish look of satisfaction, watching me bloom and unfold for him like a flower.

"You want it bad, don't you?" he taunts me in a gruff voice. "You're a dirty little thing."

"I do," I pant weakly, "I am."

It feels so damn good, and so wicked at the same

time. The rough fabric of his jeans, still slightly dampened from the rain earlier, rubbing against my mound through the much softer, thinner material of my panties. The sensation sends spirals of pleasure centering on my clit, up through my body until my whole frame is buzzing with bliss. He manhandles me so roughly, but I can't pretend I don't love it. I deserve this. How else could a girl like me get fucked? I've got bad blood. Bad genes. I'm so twisted up and broken inside that this near-stranger's brutal touch feels like a blessing. Like a gift I would be stupid to refuse.

He ruts against me, bringing me closer and closer to the edge before it dances away again, making me moan softly with disappointment. He laughs darkly, tracing one finger down my forehead, my nose, to tap my pouting lips.

"Oh, sweetheart. Don't you worry. I have all kinds of things in mind for you tonight," he promises me in a growl. "Lift your arms. Now."

I do as I'm told without question, raising my arms straight up over my head so Bones can grab the bottom hem of my gray knit sweater and whip it off, throwing it somewhere off to the side. Goosebumps instantly prickle up on my bared flesh, and I can't help but squeal with mingled pain, surprise, and pleasure when Bones dives down to capture one of my stiffened nipples between his teeth. He flicks his tongue over the peak and then bites down. Hard. I writhe and whimper underneath him, biting my lip while he toys with my breasts. One hand gropes and thumbs over the nipple of my right breast while his teeth and tongue tease my left. When he nips again, harder and sharper this time, I actually scream out and impulsively try to scoot away from him. But Bones is ready. Always. He hastily grabs me by the waist with both hands, his fingertips digging into my sides as he holds me there.

"Oh no. You're not going anywhere," he hisses, almost cruelly.

He grabs and squeezes my tits, his thumbs circling my nipples while he grinds his crotch against mine, making me moan out his name in one fractured syllable.

"Bones—oh my god," I whimper helplessly as one of his huge, calloused hands slides up my chest to wrap gently around the front of my throat, applying soft but firm pressure there.

He's cautious at first, barely pushing down at all until I start warming up to the sensation. It feels like I'm clutched in the powerful hand of a god, making myself lie prostrate and worshipful, my eyes begging him to hurt me and not to hurt me at the same time. It's exhilarating, feeling my lungs start to constrict and my body go rigid under his touch. I arch my back, leaning up into his hand. For a few harsh moments, all of my breath is caught and stolen away. I feel my body tense up, every muscle in my body straining, every cell in my brain screaming at me to gasp for air. All the wires are crossing and crackling, my whole body in a state of sustained, panicked delight. All the alarm bells are ringing. My chest aches. My stomach clenches. I feel an intense roll of tingles starting at the crowd of my head, passing down through clear to my curling toes. I gaze up into the face of the man who literally steals my breath away, staring at him like I could be meeting the face of god. I can see the little pinpricks of darkness swarming in at the edges of my vision. My head feels light for a moment, and then impossibly heavy. I feel hopeless and renewed all at once. And then, just like that, he releases my throat.

His hands rove down my body as I gasp for breath, gulping down air to fill out my aching lungs. I barely have a chance to breathe and regain full consciousness before I hear the mouthwatering sound of his jeans being unzipped. I peer down to watch him let his massive, glorious cock spring free. I lick my lips with anticipation, watching with wide eyes while he starts to stroke himself.

"I want to taste you again," I murmur, mesmerized by the rhythm of his hand moving up and down his thick shaft.

Bones gives me a look of dark amusement. "Oh, I bet you do, little girl. You filthy thing. And god, it felt good to stuff my cock inside your pretty little mouth. Shoving it down your throat, listening to you gag. But that's not enough for me this time. Oh no. I have much bigger plans for you tonight, Lauren," he promises me.

I can hardly wait. I hold my breath while he tugs down my panties and drops them aside. Immediately, we can both smell my sweet, fragrant sex in the air. Bones inhales deeply, shaking his head with appreciation. He runs one long finger down the middle of my slick folds, then lifts it to his lips and tastes me. I get even wetter just watching him. I arch toward him, lifting my ass and silently begging for him to take me.

"You want it, too, don't you?" he snarls, grabbing my thighs and squeezing them as he works his way up to circle my sensitive clit with both thumbs. I toss my head back and moan.

"Yes. Oh god, yes. Please," I beg him.

"I'm going to fuck your tight little pussy bare, do you understand?" he hisses.

I whimper with fear, but I nod my head. I do want it. I do understand.

He smacks my ass hard, making me cry out. Bones takes the engorged head of his shaft and begins to rub it in teasing circles around my clenching little hole. He slaps his cock against my flower, sliding up and down until I'm barely able to think straight. It feels so fucking good, even though I know he's toying with me. I can't wait. I'm so impatient to feel him inside me.

"Bad girls don't get to come until I say so," Bones teases.

"Please. I'm so close," I murmur faintly.

"You want it, little girl? You want to come all over my cock?" he goads me, still sliding his cock up and down my slick petals. I bite my lip and tense up, unable to hold back anymore. I come with a gush of honey, my whole body shivering and twitching.

"Look at you, naughty girl," he murmurs roughly. "I haven't even done anything yet. You must be so desperate for it, hmm?"

"Yes. Yes, please," I whimper, still twitching from my climax.

"I'll give you something else. Something bigger. You need to be taught a lesson you won't forget," he growls, and in one fluid motion, he shoves his full cock inside of me.

I cry out and fling my arms to each side to grab onto the table, holding on for dear life while ripples of sharp pain mixed with pleasure shoot through my body. He slams into me again and again, with no mercy or gentleness for my virginal cunny.

"Oh my god. Oh fuck," I whisper as he grabs me by the hips, holding me in place while his cock spears deep and hard into me, striking against this deliciously pleasurable spot far within my cunt that I've never been able to reach myself.

It feels like heaven and hell colliding, blood and come and hot, hot desire. Bones fucks me without holding back one bit, pushing past my boundaries and pounding me into the table. He pins me down, his hands pressing into each of my wrists on either side of me while his hips piston back and forth rapidly, slamming into my cunt. One of his hands roves down my arm and up to my throat, pressing down for a few seconds at a time before releasing again, every time pushing me closer and closer to the edge. I clench my pussy around him, arching my back to meet his every thrust. I can feel him tensing up, getting close. For a moment he tries to recoil, like he's going to pull out. But I wrap my legs around his waist even tighter, keeping him there.

"You dirty little girl," he snarls. "You trying to make me come?"

I realize as soon as the words leave his lips that it's true. I want that. More than anything.

"Yes! Come inside me," I plead. "Fill me up. Mark me. Make me yours."

"Fuck, you're so filthy. I'm going to claim you, Lauren. You belong to me," he quips.

He pounds into me a few more erratic times and then I feel it—his hot, precious seed spurting deep inside my pussy. The two of us gasping and spasming together, sharing the hot, humid air between us as we grapple to hold still in place while the storm continues to rumble on outside. Finally, Bones withdraws and I immediately feel his come start to leak out of my aching cunny. He hastily gets dressed again and brings me my clothes, including my jeans with the phone in the pocket.

As I'm pulling on my clothes, trying to make sense of what just happened between us, I feel my cell phone start to vibrate. I frown in confusion. It's a burner phone. Almost nobody has my number. I look down at the screen with terror slowly flooding my veins. With my heart racing, I dart up the stairs to my bedroom to answer the call.

No, I think to myself desperately. No. It can't be him.

"What is it?" I say as I see her face go pale, staring at her screen. "Lauren, what's the matter?"

She doesn't give me an answer. She just stares at the screen for a few seconds, looking like a storm of emotions is churning under the surface of her face before she looks up to me. The look in the gaze that hits me with the force of a freight train. She looks pained to speak, but she manages to move her lips anyway.

"I need a minute alone," she says numbly.

I can't believe her. One minute she's hot, and the next she's cold. One second she's making me treat her like my little girl and begging me to play with her buttons, and then she's kicking me out of her room or clamming up and going all creepy and brooding. I can't make heads or tails of her, but I have a good feeling I know what this call is about, and it's more frustrating than anything that I can see her closing up all over again after letting herself relax so much.

For a few moments, I open my mouth, thinking about protesting, but finally I just give a curt nod and head back down the hallway as she half-shuts herself in her bedroom to take the call. Once I'm in the living room, I look out the window to check on my bike before sitting down on the couch and glaring at the opposite wall, feeling tense.

Why does this always come up post-orgasm? Am I always going to have to worry about this bullshit when we mess around? But no sooner has that thought crossed my mind that I feel guilty about it, and I run a hand over my face.

Obviously, she can't help it. Everything to do with her dad and the kind of sick son of a bitch he is drives her crazy in a way that goes deeper than anything I can ever understand. And when I sit back and really think about it, she's been alone letting that burden eat her up inside about as long as I've been on the run from my old crew back in California.

All that time, I've been able to find my people. I've always fallen in with other bikers who would ride with me, get into trouble with me, and sometimes even get me out of it, if they're good ones.

Those types are rare, but they're out there. Breaker is one of the good ones, and so are the other guys in the Heartbreakers. We've had each other's backs as outlaws, and unless one of us decides to do something stupid like Buzz and his idiot son did, we won't stab each other in the back.

Lauren has never had that, by the sounds of things. I try to picture myself packing my own bags at the age of sixteen, getting ready to hit the road with no contacts, no prospects, and no knowing what the next day was going to hold. That last part was true anyway but I don't think Lauren had the other two luxuries, by the sounds of things.

Part of me wants to be suspicious of her story to some degree, but she's just odd enough that her behavior fits with the rest of her story. I'm no psychologist, and I can't explain it, but I believe her on a gut level.

I can't just let her go on with that conversation without getting curious, so after a few minutes, I stand up and move as silently as I can down the hallway and to the bedroom door. I furrow my brow when I realize I can't hear the sound of her voice, nor the muffled sound of a voice on the other end of the line. Instead, I hear her shuffling around the room in a hurry.

The door is ajar, and I stand awkwardly parallel to the hallway as I lean in and try to listen for the sounds of voice. But I can't hear anything, and I'm getting impatient, so I push the door open and stick my head in. I was right—the call is over, and the phone is lying in the middle of a pillow, sunk halfway down the soft cushion as if it had been hurled at it.

The second thing that gets my attention is the large suitcase, open and already a quarter packed on the top of the bed.

"The fuck?" I murmur as I look over to Lauren and see her pulling half a dozen sweaters out of the closet and pulling them off their hangers without acknowledging me. Her brow is knit, and she looks absolutely determined to keep working without so much as looking at me.

"Uh...hey," I say, finally stepping into the room and looking at her. "What was that?"

She doesn't answer. She stops herself with the sweaters, sighing annoyedly and glaring down at the contents of her suitcase as if something had suddenly occurred to her, and she set the sweaters aside to bustle to a drawer of socks and underwear and start packing those first instead.

"Lauren," I say, more sternly.

I see her face twist up for a fraction of a second, but she just murmurs something under her breath and brushes me off.

"Hey, look," I say, not stepping further inside yet. "I don't know what all this is, but I sure as hell hope you're not about to leave me with a giant question mark hanging over us before you withdraw again." She still doesn't respond, so I step into the room and block off her route to the suitcase, making her glare up at me with an arm full of two pairs of pajamas.

"Come on, I wasn't *that* bad, was I?" I ask with a gruff smile, hoping to lighten the mood in the room a little.

Lauren doesn't seem to find it half as amusing as me. She scoffs and tries to push past me, but I catch her around the waist and thrust her back in front of me, glaring down at her.

"Look, I'm not seriously going to stop you if a phone call from your dad is going to make you pack up and leave all over again, but the least you could give me is an explanation," I growl.

"It wasn't him!" she snaps, squirming away from me and straightening her clothes.

I stare at her, surprised, and she steps back, regarding me carefully as if silently asking whether I'm planning on stepping in and getting handsy with her again. There's a challenge in the gaze. Part of her likes that, but not right now. I can't just grab her and shake her out whatever she has going on in her head right now, she needs to be able to deal with it herself.

So, I take a seat on the mattress beside the suitcase, staring up at her and waiting patiently to see what she'd really like to do. She smooths her hair out and closes her eyes, taking a deep breath. Finally, she steps over to me and takes a seat on my lap, something that gives me a swelling sense of pride and joy. I wrap my hands around her hips and hug her to me, breathing slowly to give her a rhythm to calm down to.

"It wasn't my father," she repeats more softly. "It was a journalist."

"Journalist?" I grunt. "What the fuck would one of those want with you? Would have thought the media fiasco would have settled all that bullshit down long ago."

"There are always going to be people who want a follow-up story on things like this," she says after a brief pause. "I...I don't know how they found my new number, but I guess there's nothing you can't find if you do enough digging."

"Well, fuck this journalist," I say, squeezing her. "If anyone comes around here, me and the Heart-breakers will scare them the fuck off, how does that sound?"

That seems to get a shadow of a smile from her, and I grin at her, but it doesn't last.

"If they can find me, *he* can find me," she says at last, and suddenly, her frantic packing makes sense.

"You've calmed down," I point out, running my hands softly up and down her body. "By a lot. And I know my hands are never cold, but they're not so comforting that they can do that to just anyone," I chuckle. "Big part of that was you, sweetheart." Her faint smile grows softly at that, and she rests one of her smaller hands in mine. "You showed me a part of you nobody else has seen. If you can trust me with that, you can trust me to have your back through this...if you're willing," I say.

Without missing a beat, Lauren leans into me at the sound of my words, and I wrap her in a tight, comforting hug as I lean back slowly onto the bed with her. I hold her safe until we're horizontal, legs still hanging off the edge of the bed, and I lay her next to me to stare into her eyes with a big, stupid smile as we lay there in each other's arms.

She stares at me with lidded eyes before cuddling closer to me, desperate for comfort, and it warms my heart to give it to her. We sit in silence for some time. I can barely see anything after she gets close to me and her mess of hair gets in my eyes, but I don't care. I smell her faint perfume with every deep breath, and with her hands wrapped in mind, I can feel her heartbeat settling down moment by moment.

Her form squirms in my arms, and after I loosen my hug enough to let her move, I feel a soft kiss on my neck. I chuckle as she kisses my cheek, then finds my lips, and I kiss her back. This time, I take a tight hold of her again and grind her against me, feeling her squirm on the bed with me and bask in the comfort of each other's presence. She just feels...good, in a simple way that feels like it needs more expression but doesn't feel all that complex.

That suits a guy like me just fine.

Her hands wander over my muscled sides and up to my shoulders, where she drags her nails down as she tastes my tongue in her mouth. Our gentle, reassuring kissing is more for comfort than for passion, but there is a little of both in our every motion. It hasn't even been long since I last gave her everything I had to give her, but my cock is already getting stiff again. It can't stand every minute we spend apart, and it knows it wants to be lodged deep within her like she needs. This girl needs my help in more ways than one.

"You forgot all about this while we were messing around with each other," I say in a rough whisper into her ear. I feel goosebumps prickle across her skin when I say it, and she nods softly. "I can push this away for you. It might not be for long, but I can give you a break from your own mind, can't I?"

"So much that it almost scares me," she confesses, squirming desperately against me.

She fills me with so much sympathy every time that we touch and every time I hear her voice or see her worry. I want to comfort her and share in that. I want to beat the shit out of her piece of crap dad. And I have half a mind to give the same thing to the fucking paparazzi trying to keep this poor girl from moving on with her life. But I can't do that unless I keep her close.

"How about this," I say, holding her and stroking her hair gently. "What if you crashed at my place for a little while?"

She looks up at me suddenly, surprised by the offer but clearly interested. She doesn't seem to know what to say at first, so I hold up a hand and shake my head.

"I don't mean like a you-pay-rent kind of thing, I mean you could just stay at my place as long as you like. If this journalist guy comes poking around, I'll have the guys keep an eye out, but you'll be somewhere nobody will come looking for you. A biker's the last place anyone would guess someone like you would go," I chuckle.

"Would...would you really be willing to do that, Bones?" she asks softly, eyes wide with desire.

"Of course," I say without hesitation. "You can take your time, and I'll help you come up with a plan for what to do next. You've had a hell of a lot happen in a short stretch of time, Lauren, you need to give yourself a break." I pull her close again, putting a heavy hand on one of her breasts and cupping it, feeling its weight and shape as I grope her ass and make a warm smile spread across her face again. "And while we're planning, I can keep your mind off it, every day and every night. How does that sound, little girl?"

"I think..." she says softly, still squirming in my grasp as I slowly work my hand down into her pants, touching her soft lips and making her gasp. I start to move my fingers in small circles, grinning as I tease her while she tries to think, grinning and blushing. "God, fuck you," she laughs.

"Yeah?" I chuckle.

"I think that sounds good," she finally says, putting her hands around my face and pressing a kiss to it. "Really good. Thank you, Bones."

"Then it's settled," I say, sitting up and looking around the room. "Come on, let's get you packed up and get the hell out of here. I can probably make it happen in one or two trips."

"You're really serious about this, aren't you?" she asks, looking up at me with fluttering eyes as I take stock of the room with a thoughtful look on my face.

"Of course I am," I say, looking down at her. "What kind of man would I be if I wasn't?" I stand up and start moving around the room to throw whatever I can into the suitcase for her, and she watches me with a thoughtful look in her eyes for a few seconds before she hops up and jumps in alongside me, looking as anxious as she is excited.

And before long, we're ready to go, and I know damn well I'm getting in over my head. But I don't care.

I'd go in a lot farther than that for Lauren. We're both running from something, and for all I know, my past could be as close behind me as hers. But I can't help but notice how often she looks at her phone, looking worried. I try not to let my mind wander into dark territory, but I can't help but think…

…was that really a journalist on the phone, or is she covering something up from me?

LAUREN

"So did you decorate this place by yourself?" I ask as I lean against the kitchen counter in Bones's small, compact wood cabin.

"Yes. There's not much to decorate. Not a lot of extra space to fill up with junk," Bones answers from his spot on the leathery brown sofa.

"We have very different decorating styles," I remark, smiling with amusement as I peer around at the stark surroundings. "I like to collect things. Especially old things. I don't know why, but somehow it's comforting to me to own little pieces of someone else's history. Pre-loved items, I suppose."

"There's a certain logic to that I can follow," Bones says graciously.

We have been here for a couple days now together, and I don't know if I will ever get over the amazement of sharing a space with another person like this. I have been alone for so long that I began to think it would be that way forever. That I was so set in my ways and accustomed to the companionable silence that any company would feel like an intrusion. I am used to coveting my own space, guarding my privacy and my solitude like a dragon curled around a golden hoard. At home, I keep the house quiet. Even if I have the TV on or if I play music on my antique record player I recovered from a seedy thrift store miles and miles south toward the border, I make sure to keep my ears open to other sounds. I am hyper-vigilant, always listening for the telltale sounds of intruders. And after the life I have lived, the things I have seen, the looming shadows of people I've had to evade for all these years, it feels only natural to close myself off to the world. After all, it's not as though the world has ever offered me anything but pain and loneliness.

Until now.

The past couple of days spent in tight proximity to the strange, mysterious, handsome devil who turned up in my life out of the foggy nowhere have been life-changing. I am learning to adapt to sharing my space, to talking out loud and giving my thoughts. Still, there are some old habits from my youth that seem unkillable. I still bend and defer to Bones. I am submissive to him, malleable enough to be molded and shaped in his hands or quieted with just a simple glance. But I know now that his prickly exterior does not fully extend to his inner world. He may be a bad boy, but he's a good man underneath it all. He lives hard. He works hard. He plays just as hard, in and out of the bedroom.

It's odd how easily we fall into a rhythm together. His place is tiny, but functional, and he has little more than exactly what he needs. The kitchen is just a small row of countertops and cabinets along one far wall of the compact living room. The whole place is glossy with floor to ceiling windows, which normally would scare the hell out of me, being so exposed. But even though he lives in a neighborhood on the outskirts of Pine Haven, much closer to town than my cottage is, it still feels secluded and private. This is mainly due to the lush green woods densely packed around all sides of the small cabin. Trees far older than any townsperson currently living stand tall and proud, looming over the cabin with branches outstretched like protective arms. It's so thickly-wooded, in fact, that the moonlight can barely strain through the foliage and softly illuminate the living room.

It's Tuesday night, and we've just finished cooking and devouring a sumptuous dinner together of braised short ribs, wild rice, and broccoli. As it turns out, Bones and I make one hell of a duo in the kitchen. Well, the small strip of counter space and burners that count as his kitchen. I can definitely see how this place reflects Bones as a person. Everything is in its place, and everything is clean. He favors stark lines, minimalist decor, and high-quality furnishings that will last a long time. I can tell that he's probably purchased a good bit of his larger pieces from custom woodworkers, of which there are plenty to choose from in rural Wyoming. On the wall is a large, blown-up photograph of Grand Teton Mountain, looming majestically over the living room. There's a small, carved wooden coffee table, heavy and durable, under which lies a creamy shag carpet rug. By the door are three sets of boots, plus my one pair of shoes I brought with me. In the back of the house is the small but peaceful bedroom with its gigantic king-sized bed on a carved mahogany frame and snowy-white bedsheets. There are perfectly-cut cabinets and shelves built into the wall opposite the bed, which are sparsely but neatly decorated with framed photographs of the Rocky Mountains, close-up pictures of certain local Wyoming plants and flowers, as well as a crisp photograph of a massive, majestic stag peering back over its shoulder at the camera, caught between two deadened trees in the crunchy snow.

The bathroom is attached to the bedroom, and is surprisingly spacious for how tightly-packed the cabin is overall. There's a stone-and-marble shower and a claw foot tub opposite a massive mirror and stone basin sink. Following his minimalist style, all of the towels are a fluffy white, all an identical texture. I'm quickly learning that while Bones may come off as harsh and rough around the edges, there is a certain placid demeanor at his core. He makes me feel both tumultuous and calm at the same time, thrilling and comforting me at once. We have spent most of our time together here so far tangled in each other's arms, barely able to pull apart long enough to do the necessary bits like washing up, eating, drinking. We are drawn together like magnets, and the fire between us doesn't seem to be dwindling down any time soon.

I turn around to face the sink, switching on the tap to start washing the last of the dishes from dinner. I can hear the soft strains of a classic country song faintly floating from across the house. He has a stereo playing in his bedroom, but the cabin is small enough that sounds carry very well. As I squirt dish detergent onto a plate and start scrubbing, I half-consciously begin to sway my hips side to side, humming along with the music. The hairs on the back of my neck stand up and I suddenly become distinctly aware that I'm being watched. I know without even having to glance back over my shoulder that Bones is staring at me from his place on the sofa. There's something so oddly arousing about doing housework in front of him. It makes me feel domestic, like I could really be cut out for his. And it makes me feel needed. Useful. When you live alone, you don't get to feel that way. But here, with him, I can fantasize about what it could be like leading a normal life. Just doing all the little mundane things I've never expected to have in my world. I feel wanted here. That's something I have not experienced in a long time.

So I decide that, if he's going to watch me, I might as well give him a little show. I sway my hips more dramatically now, shaking my ass and humming louder. I let my long blonde hair swish back and forth, tossing it back so it cascades romantically down my shoulder blades. I can feel his gaze locked onto my body, following every one of my movements closely. When I hear the faint squeak of the sofa cushions moving, I'm tempted to look back, but I force myself not to. And that gives me an even bigger reward when he saunters up behind me and sweeps my hair over one shoulder, leaning down to kiss my bared neck on the other side. I sigh and close my eyes as his hands slide down my body, groping and caressing me. They slip down to grab my hips and he presses against me from behind. I feel a little thrill in my soul at the sensation of his stiffening cock hard against my ass.

I'm not wearing any panties, and in fact, I'm only wearing one of his old oversized t-shirts. It hangs loosely around my torso but is only long enough to barely conceal my ass. Not that it matters much, because Bones immediately slides the t-shirt up to expose me while he ruts against my body. He leans around to whisper into my ear, giving me chills.

"Are you trying to drive me crazy?" he murmurs breathily.

I shiver with pleasure and a coy smile pays around my lips.

"No. Of course not," I answer softly.

"Oh, really? This is unintentional?" he purrs, slipping a hand between my thighs to cup my slick, warm mound. I inhale sharply and melt into his touch.

"Why? Is it working?" I murmur.

He chuckles and presses a kiss to my cheek while his fingers toy with my clit, circling and rubbing in perfect rhythm while I involuntarily rock against his hand. I can feel his shaft thickening and getting even harder, the length of it pressing into my ass. Bones presses at the top of my back, bending me over the sink and wedging his leg between my thighs so he can get a better purchase on my pussy. I groan as his fingers slide up and down my wet slit, toying with me and bringing me waves of pleasure before he slowly, methodically slips one long, thick finger inside my clenching cunny. I whimper with desire and roll my hips, my eyes flitting over to the wide window nearby. There are lots of trees shading us from the street, but if anyone were to walk by and look straight over in our direction, they would see me bent over like a slut. Somehow, the idea of being seen, of getting caught in this filthy position only arouses me more.

"You like this, little girl?" Bones snarls harshly against my ear. "You like me fingering your sweet little pussy?"

"Oh god, yes," I whisper hoarsely, losing myself to the way his finger seems to perfectly reach my g-spot again and again. When he slides a second finger inside me, my knees start to buckle and go weak. But Bones holds me up, pinned against the sink with his hand between my legs. I push back against him, relishing the sensation of his hard cock pressing into me.

"Is this how it's always going to be with you around? You showing off and making me hard?" Bones hisses. "Begging for me to punish you?"

I wiggle my ass and bite my lip, peering back at him coquettishly. "I hope so," I whisper back. "I deserve to be punished."

"Cocky little thing, aren't you?" he growls possessively. "You better not be talking to any other man like this."

"And what if I did? What would you do to me?" I hear myself asking coyly. I know without a single doubt that there is no other man alive I would give myself up to like this, but I can't pass up the opportunity to tease him and make him touch me more.

"I would tear this sweet little ass up, that's what I'd do," Bones says gruffly. He rears back and gives my ass a resounding smack. I moan and buck against him, begging for more.

"Teach me, Bones. Teach me how to be a good girl," I beg, poking out my bottom lip.

He smacks my ass again, harder this time. Against my ear, he growls, "You already know how to be good. I'm going to teach you to be bad. Cocky little girls deserve cock as punishment, don't they?"

"Yes. Yes, sir. Punish me. Please," I manage to choke out as his hand slides around to press against my throat. I can hear him unzipping his jeans and my pussy gets even slicker with honey. He gropes my ass, grinding up against me hard.

"Keep this up and you'll be too sore to sit tomorrow, my filthy angel," he warns.

By now, I'm so turned on I can hardly think. Still, my mind manages to throw together a sassy response that I know will get me what I want.

"I'm going to be sitting on your raw cock all day tomorrow no matter how sore my pretty little ass is," I hiss back in reply.

"Such dirty words for a girl like you," Bones snarls, pressing the thick head of his cock against my hole.

I press up into him, pleading for him to give it to me. Luckily, I don't have to beg very hard. He shoves inside of me completely, the velvety tip of his shaft pushing into my g-spot and rocking back and forth while his hands rove up to grope my breasts and tweak my sensitive, stiffened nipples. Bones slaps my ass again while he slams into me again and again, striking that delicious spot deep inside with every powerful thrust. He tangles one hand in my long hair and yanks my head back so he can kiss me. The burning and stinging of my scalp, the twisted ache of my body position, and the heavenly ache of his huge cock inside me is more than enough to make me come. With one hand tangled and yanking my hair, the other pressing against my throat, I cry out and shudder with waves of orgasmic bliss, gushing all over his cock as his balls slap heavily against my ass over and over again.

"You like that, sweetheart? You love being fucked hard and treated like the dirty little bad girl you are?" Bones jeers icily.

"Yes. Don't stop. Please, don't stop," I gasp between gulps of air.

He slams into me even harder, and I can feel my ass cheeks jiggling with every push of his hips. I come twice, three, four times while he pummels my g-spot and toys with my breath, keeping me constantly on the edge of another orgasm. Finally, once my come is dripping down my thighs and his, Bones rears back and spears into me one final time. We both cry out and grasp at the kitchen counter as he releases a thick spurt of seed deep inside my aching cunt. Bones arches over my body, clinging to me as we breathe hard together, coming down from the thrill. He gives my ass one more soft slap and withdraws, his come mingling with mine as it tracks down my thighs.

"Fuck, you feel like heaven," Bones murmurs to me.

Meanwhile, I have never felt so high in my life. No level of intoxication can compete with the rush of fucking Bones. He makes me feel dirty and clean, aching and fulfilled at the same time. The two of us head to the bathroom to clean up, but try as I might, I can't seem to clear the smile off my face. I feel an overwhelming rush of adoration and warmth for him that I can't totally hold back anymore.

"Hey Bones," I ask meekly.

He turns to look at me, a new softness in his eyes. "Yes?" he prompts me.

Wringing my hands, I ask, "Will you watch a movie with me?"

He saunters over and kisses me on the forehead, brushing back the sweat-soaked locks of hair from my face. With a smile he replies, "Of course. Go on and start making the popcorn. I'm going to get some blankets and pillows and join you on the couch. Sound good?"

"Sounds amazing," I gush.

He laughs gently and pats me on the ass. "Go on, then. Put your clothes back on."

Still grinning like a fool, I pull on the old t-shirt along with some clean panties and head into the kitchen, humming along with the music as I put the bag of popcorn in the microwave. I stand there, listening to it pop as I lazily look out the window. I can't believe my good luck. How have I managed to stumble into the sexiest, strongest, most incredible man alive? I almost feel like I should pinch myself to make sure this isn't all some wild dream. But just when I'm starting to wonder if this paradise will last forever, I hear a horribly familiar sound.

The rumble of a motorcycle engine outside.

My eyes flick to the narrow passage through the trees where I can see the street beyond, and instantly my heart drops into my stomach. There's that same figure again. Ominously watching me from afar.

BONES

I make my way to my bedroom to get a spare blanket out. I've never been the kind of guy who even thought he'd have to prepare for cozy-as-shit nights indoors, but my heart is beating fast at the thought of it with Lauren.

I've been living more or less on my own my whole life. When I was a kid, I spent half my nights at someone else's house, to the point that I felt more at home when I was moving around on my own than when I was sleeping under a roof with four walls around me. Maybe that was how my love for being on the road started. Maybe that was when fate determined I'd be an outlaw as long as I lived. Or maybe, fate had just been holding out for me to meet Lauren.

All this shit is new to me, but it's good shit. That's something I can agree on with my past self, who has spent most of this evening kicking up a world class fit at the back of my mind for being all domestic with this girl. But as far as I'm concerned, he can shove his machismo up his ass. I like getting cozy with my girl, I like calling her my girl, and I like that she likes me calling her my girl.

I might be a simple man, but I can feel complicated feelings as well as I can make complicated sentences that make me confuse myself.

But as I thumb through the stack of blankets in my closet, looking for the least scratchy and uncomfortable of the bunch (which is easily a quilt I picked up at a thrift shop one day), my phone buzzes in my pocket. I glance down at it and see a text from Breaker, and somehow, I know it's trouble before I even unlock the screen and check the message.

Update: Sergeant Brandon is pressing charges against the bar for damages since nobody gave up your name.

"Fucking hell," I growl at the text, clenching my teeth. I look over at the pillow of my bed, remembering how Lauren had hurled her phone at it when she got the call from the journalist that shook her up so badly the first time. It was tempting to do the same thing now.

I run my hand through my hair and pace the room, thinking for a moment. This is bad. I don't know how long Mayor Hartley will be willing to give us a pass on the issue. He knows damn well that we can make life hell for him, but it's one thing when we rattle our sabers over some land developers the city council is courting. It's another thing for a bar to protect a guy who almost knocked out a "war hero."

Just thinking that about that fucker being revered as a hero by the locals gets my blood boiling. I know one person who *should* be seen as a hero, and she's cooking popcorn in the other room. By saving the lives of any innocents her father would have gotten to later on, she did more for her community than some spoiled would-be rapist ever has.

But I need to give Breaker some kind of answer, I can't just leave him hanging for the night. Problem is, I have no idea what to tell him. The MC isn't about to turn me in, obviously, but the longer I'm around town, the more trouble it's going to be. I look out the window into the darkness, frowning deeply

Maybe it's time for me to move on yet again.

That would solve the Heartbreakers' problems once and for all, take pressure off them in Pine Haven, and let them keep running their business without having to worry about the mayor or the police breathing down their neck. We run Crooks County, and if we want to keep it that way, we need to play our cards right and not move too quickly. We can't exactly lay low the whole time either, though. If Breaker lets this challenge go unanswered, it will make us look weak. Period.

Maybe me removing myself from the equation would solve everyone's problem. If I just skip town with Lauren, the Heartbreakers can say they dealt with a 'problem member' while still maintaining their respect and prestige in the area. The soldier boy would be pacified and hopefully move on, but as long as he's in Pine Haven, Breaker and the guys will be able to make sure he stays out of trouble.

And as for me, I'd have Lauren.

Right now, that sounds like a deal that could be a hell of a lot worse. But still, I can't just tell Breaker I'm leaving. That would be too abrupt, and I don't know if Lauren is really ready for that. I glance out the window and back down to the phone. That's a conversation that will ruin the coziness of the night, and I am *not* looking forward to having it.

Damn, someone's ego is bruised. Thanks, brother. Let me think about what I can do about this and we'll touch base soon.

I send the text and get a thumbs-up emoji back in a few seconds from him. Grabbing the quilt from the closet, I shove the phone back into my pocket and make my way back to the living room. But as I'm walking down the hallway, a strong scent that reaches my nose makes me furrow my brow.

The living room is empty. As I toss the quilt onto the back of it, it hits me that the smell stinking up the house is burnt popcorn. Going into the kitchen, I see it just as empty as the living room...except for the stovetop burner still going, and a near-black bag of popcorn smoking ominously on one of the hobs.

"Fuckin' shit!" I curse as I rush over to the nearest hand towel. I wrap it around the pan's handle and move it off the heat before turning the stove off, and I carefully carry the bag over to the sink to douse in cold water to quelch the last of the smoldering. I look over my shoulder, half-expecting a sheepish Lauren to appear at the door frame, but she's nowhere to be seen.

"Lauren?" I call. "You alright?"

No response.

My heart drops, and my jaw tenses. I'm starting to develop a sense for when something is wrong with Lauren, even when she doesn't tell me, and it's going off on high alarm right now. Once the bag is a soggy mess at the bottom of the sink, I look out the front and back windows to see if I can make out a shapely figure running across the yard in nothing but a long t-shirt. I'm not in any such luck, but that means she's somewhere in the house.

If she isn't in the living room, kitchen, or bedroom, that only leaves a few options, and staying still for a moment confirms my first thought. I hear the distant, almost echoing sound of sniffling, and that makes me think of the tiled walls and floors of the bathroom. That's all the info I need before I detour to the living room, grab the still-folded quilt, and make a beeline for the water closet.

And just as I worried, I see Lauren curled up into a ball in the tub, back pressed to the wall, eyes hollow and staring.

"Shit, are you okay?" I say as I go to her side and slowly sit down on the edge of the tub, draping the quilt around her shoulders and reaching out for her hand. When she doesn't give it to me, I frown. She seems rooted in place, so I carefully swing my massive form over the side of the tub and climb in with her.

The look in her eyes finally changes, and she looks vaguely surprised and disoriented that I've interrupted her line of sight to the faucet at the end of the tub. She swallows, looking guilty for a moment, then turns her gaze down to her feet. Her hands find the edge of the quilt, and she tugs it over her shoulders absently.

"Hey, it's okay," I say as reassuring as possible, not trying to get up in her space until she's ready for it. "I'm not here to drag you out of the tub, you can stay here as long as you want. But I can't help you unless you tell me what just upset you. Takes a lot for someone to leave popcorn on the stove that long."

She suddenly looks alarmed and even more guilty, and she lowers her eyes again after frowning up at me.

"I'm sorry," she says, barely above a whisper.

I run my hand over my face, confused and frustrated but not giving up. I scoot a little closer, close enough to reach around my legs and take her hands to squeeze gently.

"I didn't come in here to chew you out. You're not in trouble," I say assuringly, and that seems to help her...at least look up at me, if not relax entirely out of whatever episode is wracking her mind.

"There was a man on a bike outside," she says at last, and my eyes widen as my heart picks up.

"Wait, what?" I ask, furrowing my brow and leaning in. "One you recognize? Someone from the club?"

"No," she says firmly enough to convince me. "No, it was someone different. I could tell by his frame. Bones, I-I think it's someone my dad sent to check up on me."

"That's not likely," I say without missing a beat, and I firmly believe my own words.

"But it's possible," she says, sniffing and reaching over for the toilet paper to blow her nose as tears run down her face. She wasn't sobbing, but the tears were flowing, and I knew this was not a situation to take lightly.

"Your old man has spent a lot of time behind bars," I say firmly. "It would be a hell of an accomplishment if he was able to have that kind of influence despite all that, especially since he isn't part of a gang of any kind."

"He could have met people in prison who'd help him out," he retorts.

"Prison doesn't like child molesters," I say with a more serious edge.

"There's still a chance," she says, closing her eyes.

"Guess I don't have to ask why you think your dad would want to know where you are if he has the chance to get out," I say grimly, and she nods her head, still not opening her eyes.

"There's even more to it than just that," she says, taking a new piece of tissue paper to dab at her eyes. She keeps trying to avert her face, as if she's ashamed of showing how much pain she's in, and I can't imagine having to leave with that kind of repression. I squeeze her hand reassuringly and stroke the top of it with my thumb as she gets her bearings back.

"Has he contacted you?" I ask.

"Not like that," she says, shaking her head. "I mean, I think I know why he really wants to find me." She opens her eyes again and looks at me with pure, unrestrained desperation. "I think he wants me to be his last victim when he gets out."

The thought sinks in, and I have to admit, it doesn't sound as outlandish as I want to tell her it does. It's a horrible thought, and the look on her face tells me exactly how much it's been haunting her.

"It occurred to me not long after he went to prison," she says weakly. "I don't know what it was that made it come to mind, but once it was there, I just...I knew it was true. I knew he saw me as the one who got away, the one who ruined it all for him. The girl *looked* like me, Bones," she says, face going red as she's unable to hold back another sob.

But she doesn't bury her face. She clenches her fists so tight I reach over and force them open, not wanting her to draw blood from her palms. We look at the marks on her hands, and she sniffs hard.

"Sometimes I think they were surrogates for me," she admits in a shaky voice.

"Lauren..." I say, trying to push her mind away from that line of thinking. "You can't possibly know what's going on in that lunatic's mind."

"Can't I?" she says, looking up at me challengingly. "I'm his daughter. I...I know it sounds crazy, but I feel like I knew when he decided he wants to kill me next—and last. I even felt it when the phone went off and I found out he had another chance to get out. I don't know how I knew, but I saw the phone go off, and I just..."

She winces, shaking her head.

"He's in me, Bones, I told you," she says, and I feel all the progress we've been making sliding away out of my grasp. I can't imagine how exhausting it is to be Lauren.

"Well, all of that sounds like a reach to me," I say bluntly, "but let's start with what we do know. What did you see when you looked at the guy? Anything distinct?"

She thinks for a moment, frowning and trying to remember.

"I couldn't see him really well, because the porch light was the only thing that let me look at him," she says. "But he wasn't wearing sleeves, but I think he had tattoos on his arms. They were really dark. I think I saw a goatee and a really hard, square face. Oh!" she says, remembering something and opening her eyes wide. "He had this big chain-looking necklace that glinted in the light."

"Fuck," I say, tightening my jaw.

It's a reflex, and it's the wrong one to ease her nerves right now.

"What?" she asks, terrified.

"I know that guy, which might pull the plug on your theory, but it gives us another problem," I say. "I can't say for sure, but that guy sounds like someone I know by the name Chainlink. He's a friend of Diesel's," I add, my frown deepening.

It takes her a moment to remember who Diesel is, but when realization crosses her face, she pales and shifts uncomfortably in the tub.

"That's Buzz's old guy, right?" she asks.

"Yeah," I say. "Chainlink is some other outlaw who most MCs won't touch, because he's the kind of guy Buzz would have loved to have on his crew. If he's around, it could mean Diesel isn't far away."

"Isn't that good, though?" she asks, leaning forward. "Your club has a lot of strong guys, doesn't this mean you can catch Diesel more easily? Maybe?" She's clearly trying to use my worry to push hers to the side, which I'm not going to let her do so easily, but at least it keeps her from dissociating.

"Could be," I say, nodding. "But we have another problem. Our boy Sergeant Brandon McCongressman's Son is pressing charges against the bar. I was going to suggest we pack up and hightail it out of town together, but now, I'm thinking this problem might be one that we can't just run away from."

She listens carefully, but after I finish, I'm surprised when she starts...laughing? I tilt my head and smile gruffly at her as she breaks down giggling mirthlessly, shaking her head and leaning it against the cool tile by the tub.

"What?" I ask.

"It's just unbelievable," she says, staring at me. "Just a few days, and suddenly half the county is looking for us."

I can't help but grin at that.

"That's what my kind of life is like, Lauren," I chuckle, leaning back. "It's not comfortable, but sometimes, you've got to move. And when you move enough, the outlaw life finds you. But hey," I add, slowly standing up out of the tub. "That's why family sticks together," I say as I reach down to help her up.

She looks at my hand suspiciously for a moment, then gives another cheerless laugh as she takes it. "Alright, but you'll excuse me if I'm not as big on 'family values' after what I had to put up with."

"Nah," I say, hoisting her up out of the tub and

the rest of the way into my arms, grabbing her around the waist and holding her up against me so high that I make her laugh for real this time. "I'm talking about the family you make on your own in life." I lower her down enough to look at her at eye level, beaming adoringly. "The people you choose."

She blushes, and for once, her smile has some real warmth in it.

"That sounds good," she says softly.

"Now come on," I growl, setting her down and kissing her on the cheek. "I got more popcorn. Let's pick up where we left off. You need something to get your mind off all this."

And as she hops off down the hallway with me chasing her playfully, pinching her ass when I catch her and wrap her in another hug in the kitchen, I think I know just the way to *really* get her mind off things.

The wind whips through my hair as the motorcycle thunders down the empty stretch of highway leading out to the shore. The sun is just starting to sink to the horizon, melting like a pat of bright butter in a skillet. The air is chilly, but I'm properly bundled up on the back of the bike, wearing a sweater and jeans with one of Bones's old jackets slouched over my body. I can barely reach my fingertips out the bottoms of the sleeves, just the very tips wiggling as I hold on tight. I can feel his heart beating steadily against my palm and I happily lean my cheek against his back. I can't stop smiling. Even though the world may very well be uncoiling and falling to pieces all around us like a house of cards, I can't help but feel butterflies in my chest. Every moment spent with Bones is like this—warm, comforting… perfect. Except for that delicious edge of danger that seems omnipresent when he's around. I know that no matter how dark and grim things get, I can count on Bones to be bigger, scarier than any threat. He's proven that to me many times already, almost enough times for me to stop glancing over my shoulder with primal, animalistic fear. When you've lived the kind of life I've lived and you've seen the shit I've seen, it can be easy to build walls and block yourself off from the world. It seems only natural, when confronted continually with new fears and new panics to add to the roster, to curl in. To close off. It makes sense, and I don't think anyone would condemn me for doing it. Fear is a powerful emotion.

But so, too, is this feeling of pure exhilaration and freedom I feel with Bones.

Everything, from the sting of the cold wind on my cheeks, whipping my hair into wild tangles at the nape of my neck, to the rumble of the bike vibrating up through my whole body, feels like it's heightened. Like my senses have been dialed up to the highest setting. Colors are brighter. Scents are more potent. And my sense of touch... it's exploded. Each brush of my fingertips across my mysterious savior's rough, sun kissed skin feels fresh and new. It's like no matter how much of his body I discover, there's always some new angle to admire. And that's nothing compared to how it feels when he touches me. Like fire and ice and wind and rain all mushed together into one careless, heart-racing shock. I have never felt like this before. Not in my fantasies. Not in my wildest, loftiest dreams. When I look at him across the room or wake up in the middle of the night to feel his strong arm cradling me close, holding me as though he will never, ever let me go, it's all I can do to keep from giggling like a fool. Bones makes me foolish. He makes me daydream about a life I never thought could be within my reach. He gives me crazy ideas. He inspires me. And compared to the drab, gray world I used to inhabit, everything is almost oversaturated with color now. I don't know how he does it.

He's dark, but he is kind. He's hard, but he can be soft when I need him to be. He tells me what to do, but he knows exactly what I want and what I need long before it even occurs to me. He fills me with a heady strength I've never known before, and that's what has given me the boost I needed to agree to the event tonight.

We are on our way to the beach for what Bones described to me as a bonfire party. Now, I'm not totally naive. I know what a bonfire is. I know what a beach is. I've seen lots of people attend such events on TV or in movies. But it has always seemed, like most fun things, like something other people get to do. Not me. Not a girl who comes from such a grim place. I've lived in the dark like a little house mouse for so long it's hard for me to even imagine how I could appropriately interact with these fun, carefree people tonight. Usually, if I'm going to be around some kind of crowd, I need some kind of liquid courage just to get me through the door. But with Bones by my side, it seems less scary. More inviting. Like it could almost be somewhere I might actually belong.

Still, I can't quite ignore the little flares of social panic butterflying in my gut. I am going to try and fit in with Bones's crowd. I know it's silly to worry, but I keep wondering how they're going to receive me. After all, I'm not from his world. What if I can't fit in?

Almost as though he can feel my anxiety, Bones takes one hand off the steering bar to place it over my hands clasped over his chest. He gives my hands a brief little squeeze and a smile automatically jumps to my face. That's all it takes. One touch, and the fear melts away. I lean around slightly to see the beach dunes looming ahead of us. The sky is like a bonfire itself, streaks of orange and pink crossing the orange clouds. The night is settling in around us, a heavy dark blanket across the world. It will all be okay, I remind myself. I have Bones. Nothing bad can happen to me while he's around.

As we come around the corner of the highway, I can make out the smoke tendrils curling up toward the sky and the long shadows of people positioned around it. There's another flicker of nervousness in my body, but it quickly dissipates when I hear the calming rhythm of the waves rolling in and out from the shore. There's a radio propped up on a fallen tree, its branches craggy and sun-bleach and vibrating with the bass of the music playing. People are laughing and chatting, most of them holding cold beers. The motorcycle putters to a stop and Bones cuts the engine, deftly dismounting and offering me his hand. With a warm smile, I accept it and he helps me hop down.

"Hang on," I tell him with a laugh, "let me squish my hair back down."

"Yeah, the wind did a bit of a number on it," he teases.

"I don't suppose you have a comb somewhere in one of those jacket pockets?" I ask.

He snorts and shakes his head, looking at me like I just suggested we jump off a cliff. With his hands on his hips he says, "What do you think I am, a greaser?"

I shrug, unable to keep from grinning as I brush through my hair with my fingers. "I don't know! You've got the motorcycle, the blonde girlfriend," I list off.

"Girlfriend? Hmm. I'll take it. But if you call me Danny Zuko in front of the boys, I'll have to bend you over and spank you hard when we get home later," he warns playfully.

I bite my lip and lean into him. "Well, then maybe I will," I whisper.

"Bad girl," he scolds gently. He taps me on the tip of my nose and I giggle, linking my arm with his. "Alright, we ready to go now?"

I nod. "Yep. Let's do this."

"Don't worry, they're a good group," he tells me, sensing the faint worry in my tone. "They'll love you. Some of them already know who you are anyway."

"Ugh. That's almost worse. My reputation precedes me," I sigh.

Bones leans over and kisses the side of my head as we walk along down the wooden boardwalk to the beach. "Trust me, this crowd doesn't give a damn about reputation," he says.

As we step off the boardwalk into the muddy sand, several of the people nearby turn and give us a smile. They lift their beers and cheer at the sight of us. I look over to see the brilliant, confident smile on Bones's face, and any worry I might have felt before just disappears. This is his scene, his comfort zone. These are his people. And I am his girl. It's two worlds colliding, but in the best way possible.

"Bones! You made it out, man!" calls one of the men with a big grin on his face.

He's a good-looking guy with a familiar face, and I manage to put it together even in the dim light of the crackling bonfire that this is the one called Breaker. He has his arm around a stunningly pretty girl in an oversized turtleneck and sweatpants, her hair pulled back in a cute, bouncy ponytail. There's a sort of glow about her that instantly makes me want to be her friend, and I'm relieved when this couple is the first pair Bones walks us over to.

"And you brought your girl! It's officially a party now," Breaker says warmly. I can tell by the ruddiness of his cheeks that he's probably at least a few beers in, but he and the girl beside him look so deliriously happy that it makes me smile.

"Hi! Nice to meet you," says the girl, holding out her hand for me. I reach to shake it, but then she pulls me into a tight hug, to my surprise. When she pushes back, she's beaming. "I'm Kate. And you must be Lauren."

"That's me," I answer cheerily.

"Good to see you, man," Breaker says, patting Bones on the back.

"You, too. Pretty good turnout," Bones replies, looking out over the scattered crowd.

"Yeah. It's always good to get everybody out in nature once in a while instead of just packing us all into the clubhouse," Breaker laughs.

"Thank god, because I sure as hell can't get s'mores at the bar," Kate quips. I notice then that she has her hand resting casually on her belly.

"Oh my god," I gasp, unable to contain myself. "Are you pregnant?"

I immediately blush, realizing that may not have

been the most tactful way to breach that question, but Kate just nods, an ecstatic smile on her face.

"Yep! And let me tell you, I don't even miss my usual glass of wine. Morning sickness or not, this is the best I've ever felt. It's weird; I always thought being pregnant would be hard, but it turns out it's the easiest thing in the world. I already love this baby more than anything else," Kate gushes. There's a sparkle to her eyes that warms my heart.

"You know, it's true what they say—you really are glowing," I point out.

"Ah, she always looks like that," Breaker scoffs good-naturedly.

"Oh, stop," Kate says, elbowing him in the ribs gently. But I can tell she secretly loves it.

I know how she feels. Every time Bones even looks at me, I feel it. She and Breaker make a fantastic couple. It's easy to see, even in the low light. They truly love each other. As Bones and I move on to the next little group of people to chat with, I'm only half paying attention. I'm enjoying the hell out of the evening, especially once I've got an ice-cold beer in my hands to sip between laughs, but my mind is already drifting out into daydream territory. Maybe it's the glow of the moon shimmering on the waves. Maybe it's the upbeat music bumping through the stereo. It probably has at least some-thing to do with the way that Bones keeps an arm around me at all times, like he's protecting me and showing me off at the same time. Every time he glances at me, my heart does a back flip. He looks so damn good in the flickering, golden gleam of the bonfire, every sharp angle and line of his face accentuated by the orange light. I have to keep reminding myself that tonight, and every night since we met, he's mine. And I am his. It still blows my mind to think about it. How lucky I am to be here right now. I'm so blissfully happy that I even start to lose myself a little, getting caught up between the positive, playful banter of Bones and his people and the sun soaked fantasies rolling through my head now and again. Throughout the evening, I keep glancing back at Kate and Breaker. They're so happy, so excited for the future in front of them. It's strange to realize that for the first time in my life, I feel like I have something to look forward to, as well. I've been running from my past for so long I kind of forgot to imagine a future, but every minute I spend with Bones makes that elusive tomorrow shine a little brighter, look a little more real.

Maybe that could be us one day. If my luck doesn't run out.

Even the single members of the group are great fun, everyone respectful and careful with one another's egos, even as they roughhouse and tease one another. It's another first for me: seeing a group of people this big who all seem to genuinely like each other. Like one great big family sprawled out across the beach. As the hours tick by like minutes, I begin to feel a connection with the group as a whole, like I might actually belong here. Bones introduces me to two other guys from the club, named Big Daddy and Ironsides, who are both the kind of intimidating guys I would have recoiled from months ago. But with Bones there to introduce me as his girl, keeping his arm around me protectively, I know I have nothing to fear. And once you get past the rough-around-the-edges look, it's apparent that they're all a bunch of sweethearts underneath it all. Just like Bones.

After we get enough of socializing and need a break, we splinter off from the group and wander down closer to the lapping shore. Bones wraps his arms around me, resting his chin on the back of my head as we look out over the moonlit waves. Even though we've been spending every second together, and I feel like the icy fortress I've built up around myself has been slowly melting away, I still haven't been particularly open about my feelings. My past. But something about the easygoing excitement of the evening has me feeling more vulnerable—in a good way, for once. I want to open up. I want to share.

"You know," I begin softly, "I never imagined I could have a night like this."

"Like what?" Bones prompts me.

I sigh, trying to find the right words. "Like... I

don't know. Good. Happy. Like I actually belong here. I guess I kind of forgot what it feels like to have friends. Or family," I admit.

"I can understand that," he says.

"I know you can," I reply with a soft smile. "That's what makes me feel so brave, I guess. I've been trying to escape my past for so long, I never take the opportunity to just… feel things. Other than fear. It's kind of exhausting."

"Yes. It is. You can try and outrun your past, but eventually you just get tired of running," Bones says wisely. And it's true. "At some point, you just have to stop looking back."

"How? How do you stop looking back?" I ask, genuinely in need of the answer.

Bones shrugs and gives me a gentle squeeze. "By looking forward instead," he says.

"Wow. That's deep," I laugh.

He kisses the top of my head. "I know. It's hard to believe I can be this good-looking and also so clever," he teases.

I lean back into him, tilting my head back to look at his handsome face in the moonlight.

"Yeah. Hard to believe," I murmur in agreement.

In this moment, I feel complete. It's a new feeling, and not one I entirely understand yet. But damn, does it feel good. I'm just starting to think maybe my luck is changing for the better, until a loud crackle splits the air and a collective shout of worry passes through the crowd.

"What the hell was that?" Bones growls, letting go of me for a moment to whirl around.

Before we can say anything else, another crack bursts through the air, and I know with the sinking of my heart exactly what it is.

Gunshots.

All at once, it's like the world reduces down, folding in on itself at the very moment the gunshots pierce the balmy air. Suddenly, the softness of the evening spins out and frays, a harsh darkness settling in over the beach. It's like time has slowed down, a moment feeling like minutes, like hours. Everything is chaos. Everywhere I look, there are dim shadows of bonfire attendees scattering to the wind. It reminds me of when a passing car disrupts a murder of crows gathered in the street. The frantic cries, the desperate fleeing. All drifting out into the darkness and the wind and the confusion. Nothing makes sense right now.

We were having such an amazing conversation, the two of us. I was smiling. I was happy for perhaps the first time in my life, truly happy. But I should know by now I don't get to be happy. The stars were in a cursed arrangement on the day I was born. I'm a jinx. There's no way around it anymore. How many times will fate tempt me to believe I might have a chance at something good, only for it to take it right back? My destiny comes hurtling back to hit me hard in the gut. It's that age-old reminder that things will never better. And if they seem better for a second, just wait for the other shoe to drop. And tonight, it's dropped.

All of the party-goers are racing off in different directions, as nobody can quite pinpoint the direction from which the gunshots are ringing out. My eyes are wide, my heart is pounding so hard it aches like a weight in my chest, and I can hardly get my body to calm down enough to coordinate my legs to run. But then, does it matter? I have no idea which direction to run. The gunshots sound like they are coming from everywhere and nowhere at the same time. They could almost be the celebratory crackle of fireworks except that there is no glorious burst of colored light in the sky. No oohs and ahhs. No fanfare. Only screams and curses and shouts of the terrified crowd as they frantically scurry toward what they hope is safety. But in the dark, it's apparent that nobody really knows where to go or what to do. We're fish in a barrel, and the gunshots ring out one after another, barely any time to reload in between.

"Bones! What do we do?" I cry out, grasping to

take his hand as he turns toward the sound of the gunfire.

"Get down, stay down. I'm going to figure this out," Bones growls.

To my horror, he lets go of my hand and sprints off into the blackness, in the direction of the gunshots, evidently. I stand there for a second, just staring off into the shadows after him, tears starting to burn in my eyes. He's gone. Running away to face the monster instead of letting it chase him. Just like our pasts—we cannot outrun a bullet. But we can destroy the hands that hold the gun. Is that his plan? To run through a hail of bullets on the off chance that he makes it through unscathed and still full of enough fight to take them down? I'm torn in two conflicting directions, and so I stand perfectly still and paralyzed in place. On the one hand, my heart swells at the realization that Bones is so heroic as to do the opposite of logical reason, to do what probably nobody else would try. He's heading toward the monsters. Straight into their lair, without even looking back. He's a hero by instinct. He isn't afraid of death.

What is he afraid of? Losing me? Losing his makeshift family?

Is that the compulsion that propels him across the bullet-ridden beach to fight the monsters with his bare hands? He wants to protect us all. And in the doing of that, he might sacrifice his own safety, his own life, just to carry out his mission. Another crack of gunshot pierces the air and I let out a little yelp as I drop to the ground, curling up in the fetal position as though I can just sink through the lakeshore silt and disappear into the earth. I know, somewhat vaguely, that I can't stay here. That I'm making myself an even easier target by staying still. But I'm not thinking clearly. Panic alarms rip through my brain, my heart thumping so loud I can hear it resounding in my ears. I turn my head and crack one eye open to see the last remnants of Bones disappear into the night. One more huge, running step of his body and he's gone. As soon as I can no longer find his shape in the darkness, any shred of hope I might have clung to just falls out of my chest, replaced by fear. Primal fear. We are being hunted like animals, and so like an animal I must respond.

Fight, flight, or freeze?

I know I don't have the strength to fight. I would be a liability more than an aid in that regard. I've already frozen up and fell down on the ground like an opossum playing dead, and clearly this is not an appropriate long-term plan. So that leaves just one option.

Flight.

I heave one deep, lung-packing breath and scramble to my feet amid the echo of gunshots in the night. My eyes dart around, looking for any indication of safety or relief. But even the glow of the moon isn't quite enough to illuminate an obvious retreat plan. Before I can make the decision to just pick a way to go, I hear the panicked breathing and muffled footsteps of people running toward me. I turn to face them, fully expecting to be confronted with the barrel of a gun. But to my relief, these are familiar faces: Ironsides and Breaker. They come hurtling toward me with their eyes flashing, their faces wrought with worry.

Ironsides throws an arm around my shoulders and hisses, "Run!"

"Where? Where do we go?" I manage to choke out between sobs. I haven't realized until now that I've been crying the whole time.

"Just go! We have to find Kate!" Breaker shouts hoarsely.

Shit. Kate is pregnant, making her the absolute most vulnerable person present. The horrific image of bullets ripping through her body flashes vividly into my head. Thanks, intrusive thought. That's helpful, I think bitterly to myself.

"Run, run, run!" Ironsides demands, pressing at my back.

I do as I'm told, running half-blind with the two men flanking me. We're trying to escape, but we're hemmed in by the jagged shoreline. There are only so many ways to go, and into the freezing lake after dark isn't one of them. It feels like we must be surrounded. No matter where we turn, there's no easy answer.

"Where's Bones?" Ironsides hisses to me.

"He ran," I murmur tearfully. "Right toward the bullets."

"Of course he did," Breaker sighs, swiping a large hand over his face with frustration as we continue running along the water. "Always the hero. Always the martyr."

"Oh god," I whimper, imagining Bones's body lying crooked on the beach by morning.

"He'll be okay," Ironsides says quickly, glancing at me. "He's stronger than you even think he is. Don't worry about him right now. You just keep moving, sweetheart."

"Okay," I sniffle.

"Breaker!" cries out a terrified female voice somewhere up ahead. Another crackle of gunshots and the woman falls to the ground. Breaker darts past me, white-hot rage in his eyes.

"Kate! Kate!" he bellows, diving down to the muddy earth beside her, shielding her body with his. Ironsides and I catch up to them and I realize with a gasp of relief that Kate seems unharmed so far by the bullets. Just terrified. And the stress cannot be good for the baby.

"We have to keep moving, Breaker," Ironsides warns him, looking around frantically.

"She can't run, Ironsides! She's pregnant!" Breaker shoots back.

"She's got to try," he insists.

"I'll stay with her," I volunteer suddenly. Both men look at me like I've grown a second head. And maybe a third and fourth, as well.

"What do you mean?" Breaker demands.

"She can't run. I'm no sprinter myself," I explain quickly. "You two have to help Bones. He ran toward the gunners, and I can't stand the idea of him facing them alone."

"If you think I'm going to abandon Kate, you're out of your mind," Breaker retorts.

"She's right," Kate pipes up, to everyone's surprise. "Go. Run. My legs are like jello. I can't go anywhere."

"I'll carry you, then," Breaker says doggedly. "I'll carry you."

She shook her head. "No. That'll only make you a bigger target. Go, my love. Lauren and I will stay here and hunker down behind this dune. We'll lie low," she says.

"She might have a point, man," Ironsides says gruffly. "Come on, Breaker. Bones needs us. If he's going to survive this shit, he needs us."

Breaker looks absolutely miserable at the idea of leaving Kate, but finally, after one desperate kiss, he pulls away. I take his place at Kate's side, shielding her with my own body as much as I can while the two men dart off in the same direction Bones went.

"I'm so scared," I admit softly, tears starting to streak down my face.

Kate nods and reaches to squeeze my hand, interlacing her fingers with mine. "I know. I'm scared, too," she agrees. "Thank you for staying with me."

"I can't believe this is happening again," I whisper, feeling utterly hopeless. "This is all my fault. I'm not allowed to have good things. I should have known I would be punished. And now I've put all of you in the crosshairs, too."

"You can't think of it that way. None of this is your fault," Kate whispers back, shaking her head. Another crack of gunshot splits the air and we flatten ourselves down on the ground even more, hoping that the darkness will hide us.

"What will happen to Bones?" I murmur, even though I know she can't give me the answer I need to hear. Kate pulls me close and hugs me as we lie on the beach, cowering.

"I don't know," she admits. "But if he's anything like Breaker, he'll get by."

"How can you be so sure?" I whimper.

She gives me a soft, sorrowful smile. "I'm not. But when you fall in love with a man like that, you learn to accept the danger. It's all worth it, even in the blackest moments," she shares.

Before I can formulate a response, we hear the

thudding of heavy footsteps coming our way and we duck down, covering our heads even though I can still peek with one eye. The men coming toward us are not familiar. And judging by the looks of pure evil on their faces, they are not friendly either.

"Shit," I swear, trying to cover Kate's body with mine to hide her. But the men come thundering up to us with their guns slung over their shoulders.

"Please, don't!" I cry out. "Don't hurt her!"

"Stand up," grunts one of the men while the man other cocks his gun and aims it right at us. "I said get your ass up!" the guy growls angrily.

"Leave us alone!" I shoot back. We get up on our feet but I hold both arms out, trying to block them from touching Kate and her delicate pregnant belly. My knees feel like they're made of papier-mache, my whole body trembling from head to toe.

The man without a gun rushes over and easily shoves me aside to grab Kate's arm while the man with the gun starts in toward me. I freeze up for a split second, watching Kate get dragged away with pure terror in her eyes. And then, just as the man is reaching to take my arm, his fingertips barely brushing over my skin, my instincts kick back in.

Without another moment's hesitation, I turn and bolt away in the opposite direction, hearing the two men shout angrily after me to come back, to give in. But I won't. I can't. Not even now that my hopes are so low and fragile. I've lost Bones. I had to give up

Kate. And now I'm all on my own, just like it's always been. I can hear thudding footsteps several yards behind me for a minute or so, one of the men clearly chasing after me. I hear a few more scattered gunshots, which make me wince every time. Every burst of fire flashes the image of another wounded, bloody body, shot through and collapsed on the beach. I'm running blind now, far enough from the bonfire that no light can guide me. It's terrifying, but there's one good thing about it: my assailant can't see anything either. Maybe I can outrun him, or at least outlast him.

I'm no athlete, but I guess one could say I've had a lifetime of practice running away from my past. I know not to look back, not to waste time with bargaining or pleading. I remember Bones's wise words, urging me to look ahead and never behind me. My legs are quaking and burning with exertion, my heart pounding like crazy. But I don't stop. Not until my numb left foot hits a heavy stone and I wail with pain, tripping and falling to the ground… head first. My head slams into another, larger boulder and I realize I've run far enough away to have reached the jetties. I am cursed. There's no question in my mind. And if not for me, this would have been just a happy, fun get-together of friends-made-family. But I ruin everything simply by existing. My presence puts others in danger automatically. I will never escape my past, even if I run as hard and long as my body will let me. And I put others in danger, too. That's the worst part, by far. Knowing that I alone am responsible for the pain and terror of the evening. The dark realization washes over me that I was wrong to think I can walk this life with Bones. I don't deserve a companion. My life will always be terrifying. And if I don't want to watch more of my loved ones die or disappear, I have to go it alone. It will be miserable, but it's preferable to bringing everyone else down with me on the slowly sinking ship that is my life.

Still, fear is enough to propel me back on my feet. I keep running, even though my lungs are on fire. I don't look back, and I don't hear those footsteps anymore. But still, I assume he has to be there, chasing me down just like the dark specters of my past looming over my shoulder at all times. Finally, I manage to make out a watery, flickering light. Not the bonfire... a streetlight.

The road.

I summon as much strength as I can muster and start booking it toward the road. As I get closer, I see another woman about my age, maybe a little older, crouching down in the dirt. Her face is twisted and pale with pain, her hands clutching at her ankle. Even in the darkness I can tell that her ankle is swollen and turning purple. She looks up with terror in her eyes at the sound of my approaching, but I hastily offer her my hand.

"Come on," I whisper fervently.

She hesitates for a moment, biting her lip as she looks at her swollen ankle. But then she takes my hand and I pull her up. She cries out in agony as her injured foot touches the ground, and I help her put an arm around my shoulders so she can limp alongside me.

"The road," she gasps breathlessly. "We have to head toward the road."

"I know. I know. We're going that way, okay? We're going to get there," I promise her, even though I know damn well we might not make it. But when another burst of shots ring out, my injured companion limps faster, the two of us moving along as quickly as one could expect.

As we step into the faint, flickering glow of the streetlight, I can suddenly see farther than before. I stare down toward the area where the motorcycles are parked. My eyes lock onto a familiar silhouette, tall and bulky and tight-fisted. Bones. I know it's him. And just as I'm about to run to him, to help him, I see another figure come swinging at him out of the darkness. I can't hear it, but I can perfectly imagine the sound of that fist connecting squarely with his jaw. I cry out and try to run to him, blind love pushing me away from the injured woman toward Bones, but before I can make any headway, I feel a hand close tightly around my wrist.

"No!" I cry out, whirling around to face my

attacker from the darkness. I don't even get a chance to see his face properly before he slams a hand over my mouth and nose, his arm going around my neck. In a quick squeeze, all the air in my lungs dries up and I can't breathe. The world lurches on its axis and everything goes dark.

 reaker tosses the newspaper down on the conference table in front of us, glaring around at each and every one of us so sharply that it could almost make the cut on my brow start bleeding again. My face might not be swollen anymore, but the signs of the fight are still showing as plain as day, and it's what has everyone in the meeting room in a foul mood.

As for me, I'm barely able to think straight, I'm so angry, and this meeting Breaker called is the only thing keeping me from grabbing a shotgun and combing over the whole goddamn state looking for the fuckers who pulled that stunt.

All four of us are down here in the meeting: me, Breaker, Big Daddy, and Ironsides, none of us looking cheerful to be there. We hear the sharp sound of Breaker's finger hitting the picture on the newspaper's front page.

"Tell me what you see here, Big Daddy," Breaker says, tapping the picture. "Describe it for me."

Big Daddy isn't normally one who likes to play these kinds of games, and Breaker knows that damn well, so I can't imagine that wasn't intentional. And sure enough, Big Daddy looks pissed off for a second before he knits his brow at Breaker.

"Prez, one of our own got hit hard last night," he says. "What's some news story about the fight at the bar got to do with any of that?"

"Because we have to figure this shit out and treat it like a goddamn investigation, apparently," Breaker barks, sliding the paper toward Big Daddy. "And it just so happens that this paper is the best lead we have, so look at it and tell us what it says."

Big Daddy grumbles and looms over the newspaper, eyes flitting over it as he digests it all.

"The picture on the front is Bones and his girl Lauren at the fight," Big Daddy says, which is true enough.

I looks like a picture taken on someone's phone of the fight at the bar upstairs the first night I met Lauren. And by the looks of things, it isn't long after I threw the first punch and stopped him from drugging her. The angle, though, is less than ideal. The photographer took a pic right when Brandon was on his ass and I was barking at him to get up and fight me. I had to admit, from this angle, it looked a hell of a lot like there was a clear aggressor, and it wasn't Brandon.

Lauren's in the picture too, though, and I stare at her face and where it's looking. I hadn't seen her yet when this picture was taken, I don't think. At least, we hadn't made eye contact. But Lauren had definitely see me. The way her face looks in this picture, she's devouring me with her eyes, piece by piece, and obviously she doesn't look sympathetic with the jarhead on the ground next to her.

The article, on the other hand, has totally different sympathies.

"Wyoming Woman Who Accused Father of Kidnapping Enjoying Criminals, War Heroes Fight Over Her," Big Daddy reads out with squinting eyes and a disgusted face. "What the fuck is this bullshit?"

"This bullshit is what's all over Pine Haven right now," Breaker says. "And yeah, anything your imagination is filling in about what it says is probably right. I'll give you the short version: it spins a hell of an exciting little story about a spoiled brat who made a false accusation against her dad over a decade ago and is spending her time nowadays leaving a trail of broken hearts across Wyoming."

"What the fuck?!" I shout, slamming my fist down on the table and snatching the paper from Big Daddy.

I glare at the words on the paper that all seem to

meld together, and I can barely string two sentences together in my head, but what little I do catch sounds like Breaker's summary is legit. The author, some dead man named Kevin Cranston, talks about Lauren as if she's some homewrecker just out to have an idle good time. I have no idea what this journalist has against Lauren, but he seems to know her. Is this some other fucker from her past that she hasn't mentioned?

"None of this bullshit about Lauren is true!" I snap, whacking the paper with my fingers. "I've seen the hurt in that sweet girl's eyes, I don't need a grand jury to convince me she's telling the truth about her past!"

"Nobody's doubting her here, Bones, calm down," Breaker says quickly, holding out a hand to me as if warning me not to lose my cool. I have to admit, that's easier said than done when some pencil-necked shitstain is slandering your girl. "Everyone here is on her side, right?"

"Right," the other two say without missing a beat, and that makes me relax a little and give the guys each a curt nod.

"Good," I say, rubbing my face. "But what the hell kind of business does this fucking newspaper think it has, trying to drag a decade-old case through the mud like that?"

"Very good question," Breaker says, sighing. "Alright, everyone, here are the facts. That's a respectable newspaper in the great state of Wyoming, and it decided to run what looks like a tabloid article about Bones's girl. It makes her sound like some man-eating homewrecker sleeping around from bar to bar across Wyoming. And it makes the incident with this Brandon fucker look like she's just getting a couple of semi-respectable men into playing games for her."

"Bones, no offense, but how'd you manage to find the girl half the state has it out for?" Big Daddy chuckles, and I punch him in the arm.

"Worse," I add, pointing down at the paper, "it gives away where she is and mentions the Murray Smyth case by name."

"Exactly, good catch," Breaker says, frowning and nodding grimly. "Which means…"

"…that if Lauren's dad gets out of prison, there's a damn good chance he'll know exactly where Lauren is if he's even half-trying to track her down," I explain, finishing for Breaker and leaving the table to pace the room, mind racing. "I told her it was crazy to think her dad was coming after her now that he might have a taste of freedom, but this is too much. Something doesn't add up, and it's pissing me off that we keep missing it. It feels like the whole goddamn world's coming down around our ears!"

"If it feels like we're missing something, then we probably are," Breaker says. "Alright, and on that note, what the fuck happened at the party last night, and how is *this* related?" he demands, tapping the article. "Too close together to be a coincidence. It wasn't run this morning, but it was recent."

"So what you're saying is," I say, crossing my arms and turning to face the guys, "the fuckers who took Lauren might have seen this article, used that to track her down, and grabbed her."

"Exactly," Breaker says, nodding firmly. "That doesn't tell us exactly why they hit us at a party, but Pine Haven is small and everyone knows everyone. I wouldn't be surprised if they just asked around town once they honed in that much."

"That doesn't give them a motive, though," I say, scratching my stubble. "We don't know who those fuckers were, except that they weren't local."

"And that tells us something," Breaker says. "My bet is those were some of Brandon's military buddies out for revenge for Brandon getting humiliated like that when Bones put him in his place."

"I don't buy that," I say immediately, and everyone in the room looks up at me at once.

They're surprised by how quick I am to second-guess Breaker's judgment, and so is Breaker, but I have a personal stake in this, and I'm taking charge. Nobody knows Lauren like I know Lauren—not here in Pine Haven, at least.

"Then who else have we got?" Breaker says.

"Let's think about who's a problem for everyone in that picture right now," I say, spreading the news article out in the middle of the table so everyone can see it clearly. "First, we got Brandon. Local war hero people like because his daddy covers up his messes for him. Next, we got the mayor. Think we can rule him out, he was too civil to try some shit like this, and it's not personal for him, so fighting dirty doesn't make sense. Then there's Murray Smyth, who's still behind bars, and this Kevin Cranston guy clearly doesn't believe that Murray is guilty. This is a fuckin' tabloid, this shit must have some kind of personal vendetta against her."

"Jesus," Big Daddy groans as Ironsides chuckles at the list.

"But I got one more, because we're assuming that Lauren is the prime target here," I say, frowning."

"Diesel," Breaker finishes for me.

"You agree?" I ask, arching an eyebrow at our prez.

"I'm not convinced," he says, shaking his head but stroking his chin at the paper. "It doesn't fit Diesel's M.O."

"Lauren saw a rider outside her house who looked like Chainlink," I say.

"Did *you* get a good look at him?" he retorts, and I open and close my mouth, but it's too late, Breaker is already shaking his head.

"We can't rule it out though, Prez," I counter, "you know he wouldn't be above taking one of our girls from us."

"And look at your face," Breaker counters, narrowing his eyes. "If that had been Diesel and Chainlink at that party, not only would you have seen one of them, but they would have done much worse to you, if you had been the target."

"Could've killed you right there and saved themselves the trouble with Lauren," Ironsides agrees.

"But they knew Lauren is my girl," I insist, looking around at each of them. "They know that would hurt a hell of a lot worse than anything they could do to me."

"Do they, though?" Ironsides says to my surprise, getting my attention. "If they followed the newspaper to town to find either of you, how would they have proof that you two were anything more than a one night stand? How would they give a shit that you just happened to be there together?"

"Because if it's Diesel, he's watching us, and I think he had one of his men watching me *at* Lauren's house!" I nearly shout.

"Calm down, you two!" Breaker intercedes like a referee, jabbing an arm between us and glaring at us both. "There's a lot flying around, but if we can't keep our cool, we may as well pack up and leave the state now, because this is not how a club acts."

I glare at Ironsides, then back at Breaker, who's face softens a little.

"Alright Bones," Breaker says, "your devotion to this girl is real, I'll give you that. But don't let it cloud your judgment. We need to bring in all expertise we can here. That's how we're going to find Lauren, not with bravado. Got it?"

"Yeah, I got it," I growl, seeing the reason in his words despite my impatience.

"Ironsides, give us your insight on Brandon," Breaker says. "How does a soldier act when he wants to cause trouble?"

"Brandon's a spoiled kid who probably got his first taste of hardship in basic," Ironsides scoffs. "He probably has a chip on his shoulder while he's on leave, and he probably has a fragile ego. It makes sense that he's pushing to sue the bar, when Bones ruined his fun."

"That was the only way I could have saved her," I say, not willing to back down on this.

"Regardless, it pissed him off," Ironsides says. "And if his plan was to kidnap her after that anyway, don't you think it makes sense that he and his friends might try to make that happen when doing things his daddy's way wasn't enough?"

"Fuck this," I finally snap, turning and storming away from the conference table. "I'm the only one who knows this girl, and if you don't want to listen to me, then you can all go fuck yourselves, I'm going for a ride."

"Bones!" Breaker calls after me, and I know I'm in brazen defiance when I throw the door open and storm past the bar on my way up to the stairs outside, my mind buzzing as if someone rolled a hive of angry wasps into it.

Where the fuck did they get off trying to talk over me when I'm the one who has firsthand experience in all this? The guys might have their own thoughts, but I'm the only one who has spent any time with Lauren. I'm the one who'd know if someone was after her, and getting pulled in seven different damn directions isn't going to get us anywhere.

I get on my bike and roar away from the clubhouse, jaw tight. It isn't the first time I've stormed out of a meeting, and just like it won't be the last, it won't be the last time I get chewed out by Breaker when I get back, either.

The wind whips around me on the dusty road as I tear down it. I drive toward Lauren's house while I try to clear my head. I don't care that there might be a trap there, I feel like I want to punch something, and Diesel's crew haunting Lauren's house might be the perfect excuse.

Of course, by the time I ride past it, there's nobody there. Still, I bring my bike to a stop outside it, and I stare at it for a few moments before tearing away. Maybe I shouldn't have stormed out of the meeting like that. Hell, I know I shouldn't have, but I'm a man who has always followed his instincts.

That doesn't work out for the best, sometimes.

Still, I think the guys are feeling as overwhelmed

as I am by having enemies on all sides, seemingly, and I need Lauren's guidance more than ever—direct or not. So far, on top of everything I said at the meeting, I remember that Lauren mentioned her family siding with her dad during the trial. In fact, to hear her tell it, she didn't have many allies to speak of at all.

Then it hits me.

Murray couldn't do anything from prison on his own, but Lauren said that he might have made friends in prison that are working with him now. I still don't think prison would be friendly enough to a guy like Murray for that to happen, but if Murray happens to be an especially charismatic guy, it isn't unbelievable.

What if someone's helping him?

What if *Diesel* is helping him?

The dots are coming in from all sides, but these dots might be connected after all. There's only one way to find out. I have exactly one lead that I have a chance of actually following through on, and if the Heartbreakers want to get caught up worrying about the jarheads, they can do that.

I'm going to pay Kevin Cranston a visit.

BONES

In a turn that leaves one large, screeching arc of rubber on the road, I whip my bike around and take off in the opposite direction. I'm heading right back to where I had been just a few moments ago—back to Lauren's house. When she agreed to move in with me for a while, she hadn't exactly packed up her entire life and come with me.

More importantly, I had seen just about everything she came over with, which was almost entirely clothes. The clipping of the newspaper from twelve years ago I saw was not among them, which meant she had left everything to do with that part of her life back at home, if there was anything else.

If there were any clues to be had, they were going to be in there.

I pull up to the house and leave my bike as I stride across the lawn and head around back, glancing in either direction to make sure there was nobody else coming up the road. I don't exactly have a key on me, but I need to be inside this house, and I would rather not let any locals see whatever I'm going to have to do to make that happen.

Around back, I check around for any of the usual hiding spots for spare keys. People leave those things out more often than you'd think. But I have no luck, nor with the windows—none of which should be surprising. Lauren is a woman who lives on the run, always looking over her shoulder. There's no way she would leave any part of her life exposed unless she wanted it to get found.

After a few minutes of unsuccessfully trying to jimmy a window open, I murmur "Fuck it" under my breath and dig out a couple of sturdy paper clips from my pocket I keep for situations like this. A few minutes later, I've picked the lock, and I slip inside.

Everything is as still and dark as we left it last time we were here, and I have to admit, I have fond memories here thanks to her. The sight of the interior will always make me think of that first time I felt her on me, and I don't think that's something I'll be able to forget even if I have to.

The thought of having to makes me stop in my tracks, and I close my eyes a moment, taking a deep breath.

A lot of dark thoughts have crossed my mind since I last got separated from Lauren. For the most part, I've been able to keep them at bay. I stay focused, and I think about cracking some heads together and carrying her home safe and sound. The wind on my chest doesn't feel right anymore without feeling the warmth of her arms around it.

But the whole time, I've told myself I can't let myself think about the worst case scenario: that whoever kidnapped Lauren this time has no intention of giving her back.

I quietly lay my hand on the back of a chair, then let my hand wrap around one of the wooden bars and tighten, letting out the tension in my muscular bicep until I hear the grainy wood start to groan and crack under my grip. When my arm starts to hurt, I relax, roll my shoulders back, and take a deep breath.

"That's why you're here, Bones," I whisper into the darkness to myself before flicking the lights on and marching down the hallway and into her bedroom.

Heading straight to the drawer that has that damned article in it, I rip it out and set it on the bed and start digging. A quick search confirms that the junk mail I saw earlier is all "real" junk mail—it's all addressed to the real address of this place with Lauren's new name on it. Still, I glance inside a few of them to make sure they aren't hiding anything, and after finding my third coupon for half off a pizza, I decide there's nothing to find in there and look back to the article.

Frowning at it, I hold it up to the light. Immediately, I notice the black rectangles on lines of the text where she seems to have run a black marker over her name. That's understandable, I'm sure she doesn't want this getting found in the first place, much less connected to her. But this can't be all.

I look down at the drawer in my lap, now empty, and I furrow my brow. Taking hold of the sides, I lift it up and shake it slightly. Something rattles inside, and a grin spreads across my face.

"Knew this thing was too heavy to be just mail," I murmur as I take out a switchblade and pry open the false bottom in the drawer.

There are two things inside that make my eyes widen: a laptop and a thick, aged folder brimming with papers.

An hour later, I have a lamp shining on the kitchen table as I lay out the documents I've found that are most relevant, which is a hell of a lot, because I've stumbled on a treasure trove of information. The folder turned out to be stuffed with as many court papers from Lauren's father's case as she could get her hands on. They weren't in any order when I found them, but each piece of paper has been read over thoroughly at least once.

I know, because every instance of Lauren's name is censored. And the way the stroke of the marker tip flares up a little at the beginning and down at the end ever so slightly is a dead giveaway: Lauren is the one who censored her own name.

The court records detail one hell of an ugly trial, from what I can tell. The first thing I look into is some record of Murray Smyth speaking, so I can read the words right out of his mouth and see what kind of man could do those kinds of unforgivable things.

And immediately, I can see how this case wasn't so cut and dry as I thought it should be.

Murray Smyth isn't the hand-wringing, creepy-looking walking red flag I had in my head when Lauren gave me the full story on him. In fact, he's a good looking guy—just the right amount of rough around the edges for a respectable middle aged man living in the suburbs, but otherwise very put together and charming in a relatable way. He answered all questions respectfully, and there was no indication that he ever hesitated or wavered with any of his answers. He was a confident liar. He came off like everyone's dad, in a good way.

And he didn't just have a silver tongue, either. Murray had the track record to keep his fake life pristine. He spent his weekends volunteering at a soup kitchen, he jogged in the community marathon events, and he had recently gotten a promotion at work. He didn't come off as a serial killer, and he didn't tick many of the usual boxes that were signs of people like that. I could almost feel the jury's confusion about him even though he was long behind bars.

I had been able to figure out it was Lauren's name that was censored by context when I get to her earliest testimonies. Each line I read breaks my heart a little more. She was already at an age where it was easy to feel overwhelmed by the world, and she clearly wasn't ready to testify. She contradicted herself just enough times to provoke the defense into pushing her too hard, and I can only imagine the damage that did to her when she was so vulnerable.

Reading through the family's testimonies is easier after going through a separate stack of correspondences Lauren seems to have had with her family during the trial. Some of them are letters, others printed emails, a few diary entries about what someone said to her one day, and so on. And damn, she wasn't exaggerating when she said the family turned on her.

It looks like her mom was still in love with Murray at the time, and based on what all of the family writes to her, it's easy to see why: he's a pillar of the community, always been a successful and stable gentleman, nobody in their right mind would think he'd hurt a fly, blah blah blah. He was a wolf in sheep's clothing, and the whole family wasn't ready to see it yet. It just pisses me off.

She was just about to be a teenager. Even if she

had been wrong, she had pretty damn good reason to be taken seriously, and that was clear to the jury in the end. But small town politics were ironclad sometimes, and that victory had come at the cost of her relationship with her family. It's even worse than she made it sound.

I frown down at the stack of papers, looking at a round wrinkled patch on one of the pages where a tear had fallen and dried at some point. She really has been honest with me from the very start. She could have lied to me about all of it, and she should have taken one look at me and done just that. But she stuck around and opened her heart to me.

And now, I've got to show her what that means to me.

This overview hasn't gotten me any closer to finding out who Kevin Cranston is, though. Thankfully, the laptop is there for that. I open it up and find that it isn't locked, which is kind of surprising, but as soon as I glance through the digital folders, I see why. She has scanned all the documents I just looked through and backed them up here. No need to bother risking a password she'll forget, if the hard copies are right there with it.

I use it to look up Kevin Cranston and see what I can find. Immediately, I see that he's a journalist at a news journal that operates not too far from here. I even find a picture of him winning some stupid award, and I see the pencil-necked prick himself grinning as if he's not about to lose those sparkling white teeth when I get my hands on him.

The rest of his articles have the same snide tone as the fucking tabloid piece he ran about Lauren, even if he redacted her name. None really go for the throat like that one did, though. He seems to focus on the cases of wrongfully accused murderers, people whose cases were just murky enough or tampered with enough that there was room for debate. My mind flits to Murray. Kevin is definitely an annoying, shrimpy journalist, though, and that's more than enough to piss me off. Nobody talks about my Lauren like that, much less him.

I keep searching, because there has to be some connection to Lauren somewhere elsewhere. But of course, looking their names up together doesn't turn anything up. I'm at a loss for a minute, and I start to worry I'm at a dead end when another thought hits me.

I look up Kevin's name alongside Murray Smyth's.

The first page of results is vague and doesn't seem especially related, except for one link to...a university website? I look into it, and I clench my teeth at what it shows me. It's an archive of a university's page for some scholarship several years ago. It lists a Kevin Cranston as the winner of a full ride scholarship to the university to study journalism based on his essay.

And his essay was his first entry into the world of disputable murder cases: it's an independent investigation he did into the case, and he firmly believes that Murray Smyth is innocent. The damn essay won him his career. And he's using it against her now that she's trying to move on with her life. I set the laptop aside and pace the kitchen, wishing Lauren was enough of a drinker to keep more in the house.

"So I've got a motive for Kevin," I murmur. "He's a journalist, and Murray might get out soon, so Kevin wants to start picking that case back up again."

That sounds right enough, but it's a dead end. I could head to wherever Kevin works and beat his ass until he talks to me, but that would cause more problems than it solves...for now. Maybe I missed something.

Heading back into the room, I start feeling around for hidden spaces in the room, checking the usual areas people hide things. If nothing else, doing a sweep of the room will give me time to sort my thoughts out.

But the first place I search is the space between the bedframe and mattress, and the feeling of something plastic brings a smile to my lips. I wrap my hand around the phone I just found and take it out.

It turns out to be more than just a phone. There's

a note taped to the back of it, and I recognize Lauren's handwriting immediately.

B- if you're reading this and I'm not with you, I have forgotten my phone. If this is an emergency—which it probably is—I need you to call my mom at the number below. M is not out of prison yet. Details in texts.

I get into the phone immediately and pull up her texts, where I find a note to self that Murray's appeal is this upcoming Monday...in California.

A state where I'm a wanted man.

"Fuck," I growl, taking a deep breath.

My mind jumps to the bikers who took Lauren. Could there be a chance they're taking her to the hearing? I saw them head off toward the south when they ran off, but they could have been trying to throw me off. And I have no idea why they'd want her at the hearing, unless...unless they really are working with Murray.

My heart starts to race as I scroll over to the calls so that I can find her mom. But when I do, I see...no less than a dozen blocked calls over the last few days. All of them are from the same caller.

Their ID is just the name KEVIN with two big red X emojis on either side of it.

She knows who Kevin is, has his number blocked, and has gone out of her way to make sure she doesn't accidentally get in touch with him. I rub my forehead as a headache throbs at it. I scroll back to the contacts and find her mom's name listed as Sandra Whittaker (Mom—Urgent Only).

But the call gives me an automated voice telling me the number is disconnected. Cursing, I go back to the laptop and try the white pages to look up the name in the area on Murray's court listing.

Sure enough, I find a Sandra Whittaker in the low-populated county. She must have taken her maiden name back after she divorced Murray. I call her up.

"Hello?" comes an older woman's voice on the other end after just three rings.

I open my mouth and realize I didn't prepare for this at all. Fuck. What is Lauren's mom supposed to do here—her mom she apparently only speaks to in emergencies?

"Hey, Miss Whittaker?" I say, clearing my throat and trying to sound as little like a biker as I can.

"Speaking," she says, sounding cautious.

"Hey, my name is…" I hesitate. "My name is Tom," I make up on the fly. "I know this call is probably the last thing you're expecting, but hear me out. I'm a friend of Lauren's, and I'm worried she might be in trouble."

A pause.

"I'm sorry," she says after a moment, "I'm afraid you have the wrong number. I-I don't know any Lauren."

I furrow my brow. "Lauren. Lauren Smyth, your

daughter." Shit, I might really not have the right number. My mind races for something that might identify Lauren to her and prove I'm not just some paparazzi calling. "I'm not the press. I'm a friend. She...when she laughs hard, her voice kind of cracks a little at the end."

"Well, you know my daughter," says Sandra, "but Lauren isn't the name I gave her. Her name is Raylene."

"Oh, oh, I hear you," I murmur, scratching my head at this new information. Raylene Smyth became Lauren Lockett, it seemed. Raylene. It was a nice name too, I thought. "Well, look, you probably know about the appeal for Murray happening on Monday. I need-"

"Okay now, hold on, let me stop you there young man," Sandra says in a very, very tired tone that gives me a sinking feeling in the pit of my stomach. "I haven't been keeping up with the appeals, actually. At all. And I'm sorry, but my daughter and I don't speak anymore."

"Miss Whittaker," I try to say, but she won't let me get a word in edgewise.

"I have to be firm about this, Tom," she says. "I..." I can hear her taking a moment on the other end of the line, and I hold back a deep sigh. I want to be angry with her for tossing aside her own daughter like this, but I can't blame part of her for feeling pain over this. "I want to move on," she finishes. "I'm sorry."

"If you hear anything, please, call me on this number," I say. "At least do that for her."

Another pause. I'm genuinely expecting her to hang up on me.

"Fine," she breathes, just before actually hanging up.

I run my hand through my hair and stare out the window for a few more moments before standing up, rolling my shoulders back, and putting the phone in my pocket. I gather up the papers in the folder, as well as the laptop, and I pack all of it into a little backpack left behind in the closet. When that's done, I leave the way I came and march back up to my bike.

My path is clear now. It's not a path I want to take, and it's not one I thought I'd ever be in a position to take, but I don't have a choice anymore.

I have to go to California and be at that hearing myself.

For Lauren, the name I know her by, the name she chose, I'll blaze right on into the state where I'm wanted for murder.

Bright and early on Sunday morning, I pull up to the diner where the bikes of the rest of the Heartbreakers are lined up. It's the last Sunday of the month at the crack of dawn, and the club is gathered at a diner that smells like rich, fatty food and hot coffee. Breaker called the breakfast in hopes that we might not all be at each other's throats if we have some hearty patty melts and pancakes coming our way while we discuss how to tackle our problems in the area.

What they don't know is that I have other plans.

I haven't told Breaker about my trip yet, but I have everything packed in my bike, and I'm eager to go. I just need to touch base one last time here so the last note I left on isn't me storming out of a meeting in progress.

The door swings open, and I stride to the back of

the diner on heavy, dusty boots as the occasional patron glances at me on my way in. My kutte tells them all exactly who I am, and around this town, people know what it means to see a Heartbreaker.

Usually, we keep the peace around here better than anyone else. We know what's best for the town because none of us have had pampered lives. The kind of bullshit we saw with Brandon and his rich congressman daddy is exactly why we stick around town and keep an eye on things. If we leave, there's nobody else who will do what needs to be done. And that's exactly what I'm riding to California to do.

In the back room, the guys are already assembled around a large rectangular table, and a waitress is bustling around handing out coffee orders. Breaker looks up at me as soon as I step in the doorway, and we look at each other with a brief, silent regard, as if sizing each other up and searching for a challenge in each other's eyes. I respect Breaker, and he respects me, but when tensions are high, there's more to walking back into a meeting than just planting your ass in a chair.

Finally, I nod to him, and he nods back to me and gestures to a seat across from him. "Pull up a chair, Bones, we already put in a black coffee order for you."

"Perfect," I chuckle, taking my seat just a second before the waitress sets the steaming mug in front of me.

Ironsides and Big Daddy are sitting near us too, as our cluster of guys makes up the core leadership of the club. But we're not the only ones taking up the room today. There are more members hanging around the table, most of them talking amongst themselves. Skid has grown into a man who can hold his own, and he's chatting with a few prospects about his life story. Kate is sitting beside Breaker, talking with a few other members about some of her plans for the future of the bar. There's a comforting din in the room all around that makes me feel bad for taking a trip like this, but it has to be done, and I'm the one to do it.

"Your ride yesterday give you any new ideas, Bones?" Breaker asks once I'm settled, and the four of us lean in to talk.

"It got heated in there yesterday," Big Daddy admits, nodding and taking a swig of his own coffee. "But we ended not long after you left. Figured it was best to clear all our heads and put 'em back together this morning."

"I appreciate it," I say, "and no hard feelings, brother. I agree. Now's not the time to let our tempers get the better of us, and I'll be the first to admit when I need to cool off."

"I know you are," Breaker says, a gruff smile breaking through his otherwise stern face. "And that's why I'm not gonna try to drag your ass out back and fight it out with you. I'll spare you that," he adds with a wink to make sure it's clear that he's joking, and a chuckle goes around our group.

"Alright, alright, air's clear," Ironsides says, eyes flitting around to each of us. "What now?"

"Now" I say, deciding to rip the band-aid off, "I'm gonna take all this good will we just agreed on and blow it to smithereens. I'm going to California."

The three others look at me like I've lost my mind, except for Ironsides, who watches me carefully but doesn't let his face show a reaction.

"You drinking the water right out of the reservoir, Bones, or…?" Breaker asks, glancing around at the others. "The fuck's in California?"

"Lauren," I say, and Ironsides nods slowly, as if he had already guessed it. I take a long drink of the coffee that nearly burns my throat on the way down and explain. "Did some digging last night at her place. Kevin Cranston is some piece of shit reporter who thinks Murray Smyth is innocent and wants to follow up on his story now that Murray's appeal is coming up—tomorrow," I add.

"Tomorrow? Where?" Breaker asks.

"Small town right on the border of Nevada," I say. "Sixteen hour ride from here. I won't be able to stick around and eat, I need to hit the road if I've got any hope of making it there today."

"Christ," Breaker says, taking a slow breath and thinking for a moment. "Wait, you said Lauren was in California."

"All signs point that way," I say. "Kevin's running tabloid articles because he's after Lauren. He's been calling her nonstop. Murray's appeal is too close to her kidnapping for it to be a coincidence. Something's going down on Monday morning, and I plan on being there when it happens. Town isn't that big. I'll get down there, find her, and get out. And I've got to do this alone, before any of you say anything," I add, looking around at the lot of them.

"Then you've got my leave," Breaker says before anyone else can interject, and he holds up a hand to silence them. "You do what you need to do. And we'd be downright stupid to think these things aren't related somehow, so it's best that we stay here to keep watch on *this* front."

"Any news on Diesel, speaking of?" I ask. "Or Chainlink?"

"No," Breaker says, shaking his head. "I've touched base with every contact we have on this side of the state. Every ass that rides a bike from here to Casper and all down the east side of the I-25 is friendly to us if they aren't already under us. Nobody knows anything. Can't even get a bead on our buddy in the necklace your girl saw," Breaker adds.

He doesn't say "thinks she saw," either, which I appreciate.

"If we want to flush out Diesel and anyone

working with him," I say, "keeping the people on our side is going to be key."

"Damn straight," Breaker grunts. "I–"

"Y'all ready to order?"

The waitress's voice interrupts us, and we all exchange brief glances before shrugging and answering as she refills our coffee mugs.

"Let me get two patty melts," Breaker says. "Side of hash browns."

"Sausage, toast, and 3-egg breakfast for me. Over easy," says Ironsides.

"Waffle and two sides of sausage," Big Daddy grunts.

The waitress turns to me, eyebrow raised, and when my stomach growls loudly at the mention of breakfast, I chuckle up at her.

"Oh, what the hell—give me three sausage and egg biscuits to go. I got a long ride ahead of me."

She jots down our orders and bustles off with a sharp smile, leaving us to resume the conversation.

"We need to deal with Brandon, justified or no," Breaker goes on as soon as we're in relative privacy again. "We do that, we keep the mayor happy, and if the mayor's happy, things come a little more easily for all of us, usually."

"Agreed," we all say in loose unison.

"How do we plan on dealing with him?" I ask, looking around at the group. "We need to figure something out that won't hurt the town and won't hurt any innocents, either."

"I'm working on that," Breaker says, rubbing his temples. "With the kid on the way before too long, I want to get this handled *soon*. But if soldier boy loses his patience, his daddy might follow through on his threat and pull the plug on funding for development the town needs bad. That's a lot of jobs. That funding goes away, local support goes away."

"Shit, I don't like having a piece of trash like this guy holding us by the balls like this," Big Daddy grumbles.

"Me either," Breaker agrees, "but unless we can find more people that 'war hero' has done this to, our hands are tied, and the knot's just getting tighter every time we struggle."

"A knife's not a bad way to get through a knot," Ironsides suggests.

"Let's stick to metaphorical ones, Ironsides," Breaker says warningly. "That wouldn't do a bit of good for our reputation right now."

"I'll give you an easy out," I say, leaning back in my chair. "Where I'm going, I'm a wanted man."

A few eyebrows go up around me. I've never shared *all* the details about my past, not like I have with Lauren, but the guys know I'm running from something. They just don't know what. A lot of times, you don't even ask a biker about that kind of thing. It's a good way to get a set of knuckles across your jaw, if you ask the wrong person what kinds of skeletons they've got in the closet.

"Something you want to tell us, Bones?" Breaker asks.

"Not right now," I decide, putting my hands on my knees. "But what I do know is that I'm going to down to a courthouse for the girl I love, and nothing's going to stop me, not even the police. What the cops do if they catch me down there is another thing. Worst of the worst case scenarios, here's what we do: if I wind up arrested in Cali for some bullshit I didn't do years ago, so be it. And if that happens, you," I say to Breaker, who watches me with narrowed eyes, "can turn right around and inform Mayor Hartley."

The others look surprised, but impressed. Ironsides looks reluctant, and Big Daddy is hard to read. Breaker strokes his chin, looking uncertain.

"That's a big risk on your part, Bones," he says. "You know what I think about heroes."

"I know," I grunt. "But I'm no hero. I'll be there regardless. What I'm doing is giving you blessing to take advantage of the situation if it turns south for me. Unless you all recruit a damn good attorney-biker while I'm gone, ain't nothing you'll be able to do to spring me down there if the law catches up to me. Second-to-worst case scenario, I don't get caught but Brandon still has his beef with us: I'll come back up here and stand trial in court."

"That's noble of you, but I'm not going to let that happen," Breaker says.

"Besides," Ironsides says, "the mayor will just assume you won't come back into state."

"And wouldn't that solve the problem too?" I say, nodding. "If I'm not back quick enough, disown me. Chances are I'm dead anyway. Throw me under the bus and say I ran off to ride with some rival gang in Utah. Hell, tell 'em I found Jesus, I don't care, just don't get your asses burned on my account, alright?"

There's a tense silence among the four of us for a few moments before Breaker lets out the breath he was holding, closing his eyes. He sees the logic in my words. They're not words he wants to hear, but I feel much better knowing that he agrees with my logic.

If I don't come back from Cali, the name Bones doesn't mean anything anyway. Might as well put some old bones to use.

Before Breaker can officially answer, though, the waitress comes back in with arms full of food, to the delighted cheer of the rest of the bikers in the diner. Ironsides and Big Daddy get distracted enough for Breaker to make eye contact with me, and we stare each other down for a moment. It's as if we need one last battle of wills before he's willing to let me walk into something that could be my funeral.

But Breaker knows that leaders need to make tough calls sometimes. He gives me the faintest shadow of a nod, and I smile, just as the waitress sets a grease-stained brown paper bag in front of me.

"I've got his check," Breaker speaks up as I stand to my feet with the bag in hand.

"You got it, sugar," she says before leaving, and I give a nod to the group.

Wordlessly, I shake hands with each of the guys and embrace, and I walk out of the diner, ready to raise hell...and not think about the fact that I might not see any of those faces in there again.

As I throw my leg over my bike, I take out Lauren's phone to dig out the best address I can find for the town. But as soon as I open it, I see a missed call from just an hour ago, and my face pales.

It was Kevin.

My finger hovers over the callback button as I clench my teeth, but before I can press it, the screen lights up bright again as another call starts coming through—and once again, it's Kevin. My heart races, and I answer the phone immediately, hoping to take the son of a bitch off guard.

"Who's this?!" I snarl, putting the phone to my ear.

Silence.

I can almost feel a kind of surprise from the other end of the line, as if someone is holding back from doing so much as breathing. If it's Kevin, he was *not* expecting someone else to pick this line up. Finally, I hear the sound of the phone shifting against something, and I know there's definitely someone on the other end of the line.

"Listen, you son of a bitch," I start to say, but the sound of a scream in the distance through the phone interrupts me just before the line goes dead.

"Lauren? LAUREN!" I shout at the phone in frustration before jamming it back into my pocket and cursing loudly.

My blood is racing, and my heart is trying to escape my ribcage—there's no room for doubt anymore. Kevin has Lauren, I'm sure of it. I don't know how that fucker did it, but *he* must be the one working with Murray behind bars!

My bike roars to life, and in a blaze of righteous fury, I rip down the highway.

I'm going southwest. They already think I've shed blood on California soil.

And brother, I'm about to prove them right.

It's worse. So much worse than I could have ever imagined, even in my wildest, darkest dreams. I should have expected this. I should have known my fate would lead me back to this desolate place. The fate I have been outrunning my whole life has caught up to me, finally strong enough to stare me right in the face. Only, the face is not the one I expected to see. I always thought it would be Daddy who came back to hurt me, to drag me back into the hellhole he built around me as a child. I have done everything I could think of to evade him. I have spent so many long, lonely years on edge, constantly running myself ragged with fear. Looking over my shoulder. Triple-checking the locks. Listening to the silence for any edge of unfamiliar sound. There have been times when I thought he was close.

One day, years ago, when I lay in my bed at night staring up at the whorls and peaks of the popcorn ceiling. Finding shadowy faces in the spackle and thinking up lives for them to lead. Characters in a world I could never touch, out in the free air, making friends and falling in love, moving ahead with their lives and following their dreams. I used to sometimes imagine myself as one of them. Just another normal young woman with a bright future ahead of her. The possibilities were endless when I thought about it that way. I could make believe for a little while that I would not wake up alone forever. That one day I might wake at the soft tendrils of dawn filtering through the window to caress my cheek, to open my eyes and reveal the sleeping angel beside me. Always there. Right nearby to look after and protect me from the shadowy ghosts that have tracked my every step since that fateful day when I found Sandra cowering in the garden shed out back. I could pretend like that was someone else's life, someone else's trauma. If I could just shift the burden for a little while and let my body stand tall and free and unobstructed, what monumental things could I carry?

Friendships? Family? Love?

A child?

Maybe someday, I always told myself. Someday I would shrug off the weight. Someday I can live in the real world and be a functional member of society. I can do all the simple things, the easy things like going to the grocery store alone and perusing every aisle for goodies instead of rushing in with my bare-bones list clutched in my trembling hands, my eyes wide open and eternally scanning for the face of the man who haunts me.

My father. He's been behind bars for years, but I should have known the justice system would not keep him from hurting me, even from a remote location. It's like he's got this secret direct line to my triggers, like he can pull any number of cords and manipulate me like a marionette. And even though his hands have not been able to touch me through the void between us, I'm still not free of his power. Because now he has a proxy. A minion to carry out his evil plot against my sanity and safety.

Kevin Cranston. That damn reporter already known for pushing limits and crossing boundaries. I suppose it only makes sense. Of course he would be behind this. He's reached new levels of psychotic. I always thought he was like a buzzing fly in my face, a constant annoyance but nothing more serious than that. I thought wrong. So wrong. He's not a buzzing fly, he's a wasp, ready to sting at any time on the behalf of my father. I don't know how it happened, how the wires in his head must have gotten crossed. He used to write scathingly of my father even when he defended him. There must have been a time years ago when Cranston still thought of my father as a bad man, albeit wrongfully accused in this particular case. But his contempt for him has mutated into sympathy, then admiration, then obsession. And now he might as well be yet another puppet in my father's show.

And I am the one who brought Daddy down. That makes me Cranston's enemy.

Because Cranston is obsessed with Murray Smyth. With me. And he will stop at nothing to finish the job Daddy started if he's not let out on compassionate release on Monday. That's why Cranston kidnapped me and brought me here. To hold me for him. I don't know how long I have been here. It must have been days. Cranston did...something to me. To my mind. It feels so cloudy, like it's difficult to string together two thoughts. I have been cowering here in the darkness in a complete daze, unable to work out how I ended up here or how the hell to burst free. And every time I think of getting out, all that comes to mind is Bones.

Will I ever see him again? Is this is the end of our barely-bloomed love story? Is that short, glorious time we spent together going to be the completion of my romance? I can't help but feel cheated. I have given so much time to my father, who menaced me. My mother, who didn't believe me. Who betrayed and abandoned me. And Sandra's face, the way she looked at me so desperately when I stumbled across her in the dark shed. The way her eyes reflected back the same hopelessness and dread I have carried ever since that day. The way she looked like a mirror image of me, only broken apart inside. I think now I am broken enough to match her. My father would be pleased: two of us, identically scarred by his evil intentions. Double the fun. Double the torture. It's a sickening thought that makes my stomach lurch. I always blamed myself. If I had a different face, a different body, if I didn't linger when I hugged my father or crawl into bed with my parents when a nightmare haunted me too much to lay alone in my childhood bed. Perhaps I taunted him too much every day of my existence. Maybe he had been courting and grooming me since the day I was born.

He wanted to mold me into the perfect victim. And I would have been. I trusted him implicitly, without question. Why wouldn't I? He's my father. I grew up believing my parents, even though they weren't perfect, were on my side. That they could always be counted on to protect me from the darkness in the world.

But the darkest place in the universe was right under my nose all along. The backyard. I remember the way the dead grass crunched under my feet. The smell of pine sap on the air. Clouds moving slowly across the gray sky above. A bird in its nest chittering at me, warning me to stay away. I remember feeling lighthearted, thinking there would be baby birds soon, chirping and fluttering their silly little featherless wings. There was even a smile on my face when I walked into the darkened shed, but it quickly faded when my eyes fell on Sandra. So similar to me and yet different. Older, somehow, even though she was my exact age. Daddy would not have had it any other way. She needed to be a replica of me, of the victim he couldn't have. But her time in captivity aged her. I wonder if my father saw that, if it disgusted him. After all, he wanted me the way I was —innocent, naive, totally trusting. Sandra lost her innocence the moment he kidnapped her and closed her off in that damn shed.

I might know how she feels now. I spent years in a metaphorical shed of my own device, trying to keep the shadows at bay. But now? Now I really understand. I, too, have been unceremoniously shoved into this dark, small space. It smells so musty and wet, like the years have done a number on it. And through that scent, something else. Something so faint but familiar that it makes my heart skip a beat.

Pine sap. The scent of my childhood as I ran across the brown and green needles on the ground, playing and laughing in the cold air as the wind whipped my hair and made my eyes water. The smell is so inextricably linked to my youth that I feel the years peeling back. Time reverses, shuffling me back through the hallway of memories that led me out of that horrible shed, putting me back in the shoes of the little girl I was when I first found Sandra. And it smells just like this. It feels just like this.

"No," I murmur, hardly able to breathe.

I walk over to the side of the room and press my hands into the mottled, humidity-worn wood. If I peek through the one tiny crack that lets in a single skinny finger of light from the outside, I can see it— the great, big pine tree I used to play underneath. The mossy spot in the sun where I used to lie down with a book and get lost. Just yards away from the shed. I was clueless back then. But not now.

I know exactly where I am.

I'm home. In the same shed where Sandra was locked up. The impostor is long since freed, but the original? I'm here now. Right where Cranston wants me, which is right where Daddy wants me.

All of the things that used to fill this place have been removed. Some of it collected and bagged by the police team as evidence in the case against Murray Smyth. Others of them picked out of the wreckage and sold off to pay all the bills my mother owed, the bills she blamed me for incurring, as well. It was always my fault. I was too desirable and yet not useful enough. I was costly. I was difficult. I came with a price tag, and my mother did not want to pay it. She didn't want to believe the story, even though it wasn't just mine. It was the story the cops followed, the news promoted, and reporters like Kevin Cranston flocked to it. I guess it was just too difficult to accept that her husband was a bad man. I guess I can't blame her too hard for that. I can hardly imagine something more heart wrenching than learning that the man you love, the father of your child, is a demented criminal.

Kevin must have bought the house, the shed along with it. I don't think he had to pay much to get it. My mother sure as hell didn't want anything to do with it once my father was arrested, so we left. And in our part of the world, this address is seared into local memory. Nobody would want to buy the old Smyth house. Nobody but Cranston.

Suddenly, a burst of fear and adrenaline seizes me. I can't stay here much longer if I want to keep my sanity. I rush to the door and start to bang my fists on it, crying out.

"Let me go! Help! Please!" I shout desperately. But no help comes.

Nobody comes at all until a few minutes later, once I've slumped against the door hopelessly. I quickly jump up and stumble back as the door creaks open and a large male figure slinks inside. I cower against the back wall, my heart pounding. The man moves closer and closer, until that one tiny shaft of light illuminates his face. My stomach turns. It's him.

"Mr. Cranston," I whisper.

"That's right. You remember me," he says, with a prideful smirk. "Good."

"Why are you doing this?" I beg.

"I don't have a choice. There's only one way. You are the girl who ruined Murray Smyth's life and reputation. You deserve to be punished. To be finished off," he relays.

I swallow hard. "How long are you going to keep me here?" I mumble.

"As long as it takes. But don't be impatient, darling. I have waited a long time to bring you here. Let's not rush things," Cranston says, as though he's talking about a vacation or something instead of kidnapping and, probably, murder.

"I don't understand. There were so many people at the bonfire. How did... how did you get me?" I ask, dreading the answer.

He scoffs and folds his arms over his chest. "It was easy. Just a few whispers in the right ears and suddenly, you have a whole lot of enemies you don't even know about," he jeers. "Don't get me wrong, it's been a long time coming, and a lot of work. So much to set up. My to-do list was so long. But I stayed true to my mission. I set it all up. I pretended to be you, Lauren, on the internet. Turns out, there's no better bait than a beautiful virgin. I became you. I posted on forums about wanting to fulfill a dark fantasy of getting roofied and assaulted. Some girls are bad like that. I assume you might as well be, too. And the guy fell for it: hook, line, and sinker. Oh, what's the bastard's name? Ah! Brandon."

"What?" I gasp.

Cranston nods proudly. "Yes. I tempted him to that clubhouse. To watch you. To want you. He was going to attack you. And I was going to save you."

"You mean kidnap me," I retort through clenched teeth.

He shrugs flippantly. "Eh. Semantics. But my perfect plan was foiled. That stupid man stepped in and took you away before I could," he sneers.

"Bones. He saved me from the both of you," I put it together.

"Right. So he became a target, too. I wanted to teach him and his stupid friends a lesson. That's why I fired all those shots at the beach party. Just to cause a little mayhem. Scare the hell out of them. But then… through the chaos, I saw it: my golden opportunity. You were there, and you were virtually alone," he says, eyeing me greedily. "I decided there was no better time than the present. I nabbed you. And now you're mine."

"You're insane," I hiss.

"I'm brilliant," Cranston shoots back defensively. "Nobody will be looking for you. You see, I planned it all out so perfectly. Everybody suspects it was just a rival biker gang who fired shots on your little crew of misfits at the beach."

"How do you know that?" I demand tearfully.

"Come on now, Lauren. You don't think I'm a complete imbecile, right?" he coos. "I did my research. I know that a man called Diesel has a feud with your filthy Heartbreakers. All I had to do was give Diesel the right information and he followed through beautifully. Just as I expected. People are so simple, Lauren, once you boil them down to their greatest desire. He wanted revenge, and conveniently enough, so do I."

I stare at him with pure horror. I can tell he's thought this through. He's been careful and deliberate all along. But I remind myself that I am not a little girl anymore. I can stand up for myself. I can get information out of this guy if I just work it right. I don't have to just be afraid. I can be smart about this.

So, without changing the terrified tenor of my voice, I ask, "And my father? What about him? How is… his case going?"

Cranston's eyes brighten as he warms to his favorite subject.

"It's likely he will finally be released on Monday," he admits. "And then he'll come home to finish what he started. Oh, I can hardly wait. It's been so long, Lauren. You're not a scrawny child anymore. You're even better. A beautiful woman with curves. Womanly features. Your father is going to be so pleased when he sees you."

I fight back the revulsion rising in my chest and ask him, "Will you be taking me to my father's favorite hunting spot, then?"

"Oh no," he laughs derisively. "No need, darling. You're already home."

BONES

My eyes are narrowed and hawklike as I speed down the dusty desert highway on my motorcycle. The roar and rumble of the engine is the loudest sound for miles and miles in any direction, maybe even the only sound. I turn my head from left to right, taking in the desolate surroundings I have been driving through for hours. It's strange; this part of the world is sequestered away between several large cities. Vegas, Salt Lake City, Sacramento. None of these big cities are entirely out of reach. They're only a few hours' drive away if you travel hard and light. And yet this stretch of desert seems ancient and separate, like a secret city built by hands of a long-lost civilization. Everything is quiet. Everything is flat and barren for as far as the eye can see. The reddish clay earth dries and cracks like chapped skin, only now and again broken up by a pattern of low, prickly shrubs.

There is nothing hospitable about the world out here. This is not a place that fosters great ideas or great minds. I can see why Lauren's old hometown has been gradually dwindling away to a ghost town all these years. I can't imagine why anyone would choose to live out here, on the bare border between Nevada and California, the red rock formations rising like watchful giants now and then in the distance. It is so quiet and empty, and yet I feel the distinct sensation of being watched. The hairs on the back of my neck stand up. My hands tighten over the steering bars until my knuckles go pearly white with tension. I have to keep reminding myself to stop clenching my teeth. It feels as though at any moment, I could turn my head and barely catch someone looking over my shoulder. Just a glimpse. A shimmer of mirage that disappears when you look directly at it. This land feels heavy with ghosts, with dead-end dreams that never even got off the dusty ground. Bad things happen here. I can't help but wonder morbidly if the reddish dirt is stained that color with years of spilled blood.

And when I start to roll through the outskirts of town, it only gets worse. This place is barely breathing these days. People have realized there is much more to the world than suffering in claustrophobic silence in the town where you were born.

Nobody chooses their birthplace. And if they could, they sure as hell would not pick a place like this. Your past, your origins are out of your hands. But your future—that belongs to you. Nobody wants to live out their future here, and I don't blame them. Every building I ride past is in some degree of dilapidation and abandonment. The old downtown saloons and hair salons and diners sag under the oppressive glare of the desert sun. The windows are either shuttered or smashed, with glittering bits of broken glass shards all over the weedy pavement. There are potholes and disintegrating sidewalks, brick foundations crumbling to dirt with the weight of propping up a town which has been dead for a long time. I cannot imagine there was ever a time when this place was a desirable location. I suppose at some point it must have had something to offer, or people would never have attempted to build a town in a hellscape like this. And if they were so inclined to live here in the first place, despite the isolation, despite the hostile climate, then what could it have been that drove them out in the end?

I have to wonder if it has something to do with the murders.

That seems like a fair enough reason to abandon your home, your memories. Once they've been stained with someone else's blood, what good are the sepia-toned recollections of a youth spent desperately searching for something to pass the time, in a world that has little to offer and every-thing to take. I pull over to the side of the bumpy, unmaintained road for a moment, the engine idling while I take out the well-worn road map I brought with me. I unfold its fraying pages and my eyes scan the lines of highways and small residential streets until they land on the money spot—the address of Lauren's old childhood home. There it is, circled in bloody red. I look up and around. This is the down-town area, where businesses once survived (I can't imagine they flourished, but at least survived for a while). This is the hub of activity. And yet, no matter where I look, I see only degradation and desolation. No stir of car engines. No chattering families down-town for a good afternoon of shopping and dining out. There is nothing left here to suggest life has gone on after whatever death it was that took the town down with it.

I am not a man who is easily spooked, but even I have to admit this is one hell of a ghost town. With renewed confidence in my directions to Lauren's old house, I start up the engine again and roll out onto the main road through town. As I drive through, I continue to tally up the number of dead, scraped-out husks of old public buildings and homes. It looks almost as though some horrific natural disaster has cut through here, but I know that's not what killed the town. Not here. Disaster isn't necessary; this place was doomed from its conception.

I make a few turns, every now and then catching sight of a light on in a window, telling me that there are still some stragglers stubbornly trying to stick it out here in desert purgatory. I hesitate to call them brave souls. More foolish than brave, I would say. But I have to give them some credit for managing to survive in a town that has long stopped supporting them back. I follow the road map image in my head until finally I roll up to the front of a small, sagging bungalow with a crooked, damaged roof and a very unsafe-looking front porch. The front steps are missing a stair, and the windows are nearly black with dust and grime. The house looks utterly cursed and clearly abandoned. But I can tell by the broken, rusted tricycle lying on its side in the driveway that it wasn't properly cleaned out when its tenants moved on.

"Oh, Lauren. What a shitty start to your life," I murmur grimly to myself as I turn off the bike engine and slide off to walk up the crooked driveway.

I look around just in case there are any nosy neighbors watching me about to break into an empty old home, but I don't see anyone around. In fact, this whole street might as well be torn down. There are no signs of life to be found here. In the red-dust front yard filled with cracked and parched brown grass, there is a rusting FOR SALE sign sharing a stake with NEW PRICE! It only adds to the forlorn appearance of the place, especially because anyone in their right mind would know this place will never sell. Nobody wants to live here. There is something dark and ominous in this house, like the filthy windows are a pair of unblinking, vigilant eyes.

I deftly climb up the broken front steps onto the creaky front porch with its missing planks and gaping holes. I move cautiously up to the front door and listen closely, holding my breath. There's no sounds from within, just as expected. Still, I'm not totally keen on the idea of just bursting into this abandoned old house just yet, so I take out my cell phone and decide to attend to some other business first. I dial the number for Ironsides, listen to the line ring twice, and then he picks up.

"Yeah?" he answers in typical gruff fashion.

"Any new leads on the frat guy situation?" I ask in a lowered voice.

"You mean Brandon? Yeah. I talked to the guy. Real skeevy kid. Skittish like a little weasel. I don't like him," Ironsides says.

"And? Did he listen to reason?" I prompt him.

"Sure did. We came to an, uh, agreement," he replies.

"What about Lauren?" I ask. "Was she around there?"

"No. No sign of her. And Brandon, dumb as he may be, seemed to be telling the truth about this mess. He has no idea about anybody getting abducted. That's not the topic we met up to discuss, though," he relays.

I groan and pinch the bridge of my nose. "Alright. Well, did you at least convince him not to press charges?" I ask.

"Eh, we'll figure that out when you get back here, yeah? That's not important right now. You went out there to find your girl, right?" Ironsides says.

"Yes," I sigh.

"Good. Keep looking. Focus on that. We're busy back here, too, looking for Diesel and his slimy gang," he grunts.

I can feel anger rising in my chest. I'm impatient. I want all the shattered pieces of this mess to fall into place already so I can find Lauren and get her back to safety. But I know Ironsides is right: I need to stay focused on the task at-hand and keep my rage at a safe distance. I need to remain calm. I have to do this right.

"You good, man?" Ironsides says, shaking me out of my thoughts.

I clear my throat. "Yeah. Yeah, I'm good. Listen, I'm standing on the front porch of Lauren's old house she grew up in. I've got to go," I explain.

"Say no more. Go ahead. Just be careful. That place may be a ghost town but you still don't want a breaking and entering charge over your head," he warns.

"Got it. I'll be careful," I tell him. "Talk later."

"Yep. Later," he says, and the line goes dead.

I slide the phone back into my pocket and tentatively try the front door knob. I fully expect it to be locked, but to my surprise, the door just creaks open. I am instantly hit square in the face with a putrid smell and I wrinkle my nose as I step through the threshold.

This place is a damn pigsty. Books with pages ripped out. Clothes stained and holey draped all over the floor and dusty, moth-eaten furniture. A cockroach scurries away from my heavy footsteps to take refuge under a sagging lounge chair. The place looks even smaller and more cramped on the inside than it appeared on the outside. I can't imagine a lot of positive memories happening in a house like this, even before it was abandoned. These people left in a hurry, that much is clear. They didn't pack up well. The house is still littered with stuff, as though they only took some clothes and valuables and hightailed it out in a rush. On the molding rug there's a doll with one glassy eye missing, the other half-lidded and staring right at me. Her plush little body is naked, a fly crawling on her porcelain cheek.

I walk through the foyer to the little kitchen area. There are still pots and pans on the stove, dishes collecting mold and grime and flies in the parched sink. I have to cover my face to walk through it, the smell is so foul. I step into a small living room, where an empty entertainment center takes up the bulk of the space. There's a red velour sofa stained and sticky with age. The pillows are ripped open, with little bits of cottony fluff scattered across the creaky floorboards. On the coffee table, caked with years of thick dust, is what looks to be a scrapbooking binder or maybe just a photo album. I gingerly pick it up, feeling the dust sink in under my fingernails as I open the front cover and begin to flip through. It is a photo album, but only a sparse number of photographs are in here. Most of them depict Lauren's father and mother, only rarely showing photographs of Lauren herself as a child. And to my horror, I realize that in the majority of those, Lauren's sweet little childish face has been burned out, probably with a cigarette. It fills me with rage to know how unfairly she was treated, how little her own family thought of her. It amazes me how strong and kind and resilient she has become, despite the terrible upbringing she suffered through. These people, her supposed parents, gave her nothing to go on. They did not prepare her for the world. Hell, they didn't even protect her from it. I shake my head, clenching my teeth and fists with bitter anger.

I feel a strong sense of resolve for my mission once again. I have to save her. Nobody else will. She just has to hold on and stay strong a little longer. I *will* find her and I will set her free. I only hope I can get to her in time.

I set down the photo album and think for a moment. Where should I look next? I recall Lauren telling me briefly about the shed out back where her slimeball of a father kept his young victims captive. I stomp through the house to the back, scraping the sliding glass door open to step out into the blistering desert sun. In the back corner of the yard, sure enough, surrounded by years of stacked pine needles in varying shades of red, brown, and green, is a shed. However, I can tell by the positioning of the shed that it must have been removed for a time and then brought back. I don't know if it was the police that did it or somebody else. Either way, it's there.

I notice then that even though I can't hear anything amiss, there are relatively fresh tracks on the ground through the pine needles and sandy mud. With adrenaline starting to pump through my veins again, I take out my gun and slowly begin to approach the shed. I stop at the door for a brief moment, looking around to make sure nobody can see me. It's dead and empty out here. Quieter than a tomb. So with no further hesitation, I clutch my gun and kick down the door.

BONES

The door nearly splinters and disintegrates under the force of my kick, showing its age and degradation. A puff of dank, musty air leaks out of the door, filling my nose with the acrid scent of dark intentions and unmeasured evil. Again, I feel the hairs on the back of my neck stand up, my skin growing goosebumps as I squint into the near-pitch blackness of the shed. I glance around one more time for safe measures, and then I step inside, ducking under the low entryway. The place looks and feels empty, just as abandoned and isolated as the rest of this ghost town. I can feel sorrow and pain leaks through the walls. Spiders scurry and spin on their webs in the corners. Little bugs skitter away from my impending footsteps, disappearing back into the warm, wet safety of the dark. There does not seem to be any sign of life beyond these insects and arachnids. A whistling wind blows around the shed like a wailing witch, adding another aspect of creepy desolation. I take a few more small steps inside, careful not to let the door shut behind me. Although, I think to myself with a wry smile, I kicked the damn door in so hard I doubt it will even fit on the hinges properly anymore, much less have the capacity to automatically lock from the inside out like it was clearly designed to do.

I can't help but look around in the shadows and imagine the horrors that went on in here. Murray Smyth was one sick, demented man. The idea that he would have tortured and abused innocent little girls in this place is more than enough to lend it a level of unease and perversion. Bad things have happened in this place. This ground is probably stained with the blood of the naive, the soft, the more harmless and helpless of us all. My hands curl into fists at the thought of Murray Smyth luring a little girl into danger. I wonder how he did it. Did he offer them something in exchange for giving up their safety? Candy? Money? Most of the little girls who grew up in this godforsaken town must have struggled from the very start. It's a food desert, and jobs are few and far between. I bet all of his little victims hailed from similarly strapped families. They would have known, on some level, that their parents were struggling to pay rent, to keep the lights on and the water running. Smyth preyed on the most vulnerable among us, weeding them out and separating the calves from the crowd like some perverted wild predator. Only instead of hunger guiding his hunt, it was some sick pleasure in hurting others.

I shudder and have to remind myself to unclench my teeth and fists. This shit just makes me so damn angry. How can a man call himself a man when he carries out such hideous acts against helpless children? I am no stranger to darkness. I know precisely the kind of trouble a man can cause. I have lived on the border of dark and light for a long, long time now. And yet, the kind of evil represented in Murray Smyth is one I do not understand. I don't even want to understand it. I just want to stamp it out and kill it so it never has to happen again.

Strangely enough, just as I'm thinking about that shithead, I hear the crackle of a small ham radio starting up and then cutting off again. I look around in confusion and my eyes land on a small wooden work bench, on top of which sits the ham radio. I bend down and switch the thing back on. It feels like it was left here for a reason. It might be a trap, but it could also be a clue, so I'll bite at this bait. There's a moment of harsh violin music and then a muffled, garbled male voice speaking in the kind of halting tone you get when someone is reading off a cue card. Almost as though possessed, it begins to fashion its staticky sound into words.

It doesn't take more than a few seconds for me to

realize with a jolt that it's a live feed of Murray Smyth's appeal trial. The defense lawyer, scumbag that he must be, is giving an impassioned sob story about how his client was wrongfully accused.

"Ladies and gentlemen of the courtroom, you have to listen closely to what I am about to tell you all," he begins. I can almost picture his smug, punchable face as he speaks. I can see him pacing back and forth with his hands behind his back and an accusing glare in his eyes.

"My client, Murray Smyth, has become a household name. Not for his work or his positive achievements throughout his life, but for the ways in which his good name has been slandered clear from here to across the world," the defense attorney explains. "For many long years, this man has been held in prison, at the mercy of the unfeeling guards and his vengeful fellow inmates. Do you know, my friends, what happens to men incarcerated for child abuse or pedophilia? Do you know how many times my client has been beaten and punished for a crime he did not commit? The first time he was attacked was right here, in this courtroom, when a jury convicted him of crimes he has nothing to do with. That was the first strike. The first blow."

"Oh, come on," I murmur impatiently.

"Now, I don't have to fill you in on everything that has gone wrong, although you can rest assured that the judicial system has routinely made mistake after mistake in this case," the lawyer claims. "You have all heard about the DNA found at the scene, about how it broke the case and removed any shadow of a doubt about my client's guilt. But I am here today to tell you that you have been purpose-fully misled. That DNA, which greased the wheel for the prosecutors to shuffle my client off to jail, could very well have belonged to Smyth's daughter, who also spent time at the scene of the supposed crimes. This was never mentioned in the trial. Ask your-selves, why is that? Why was such a crucial aspect of the DNA evidence completely left out of the public record? And on top of that, you have to question why the DNA was such a surefire proof in the first place. After all, the shed did belong to my client, Mr. Smyth. He spent time there. It was his work shed. It makes sense that his DNA would be present at the scene, but it does not automatically mean he is guilty of the crimes that took place there."

The lawyer pauses as a titter of soft conversation and surprise ripples through the courtroom. I feel that old rage swelling up inside of me again. How could these people be so stupid? So easily led astray? Can't they just look at Murray Smyth's dead, dark eyes and tell there's no soul knocking around inside of him? Can't they listen to the evidence collected and know without a doubt that he is a guilty, perverse man? How can they let this quick-talking lawyer put questions in their heads? He has them right where he wants them. Eating out of the palm of his hand, totally unaware that he's feeding them poison. He goes on.

"And let us also remember that Mr. Smyth's wife, the mother of his child, still supports her husband after all these years. Think about that for a second. Do you think a level-headed woman in her right mind would ever continue to support and advocate for her husband if she had any inkling that he might be involved in such disgusting affairs?" the lawyer points out. "How many times have we heard the story of the husband committing a heinous crime and the wife turning against him? It's an age-old story. I can tell you, as a defense attorney with a lot of years under my belt, it happens all the time. People take sides. People defend who they believe to be telling the truth, even in the face of courtroom condemnation," he says.

Wow, this guy sure loves his alliteration. And his bombasting.

"But my client's wife believes him. She stands with him, even after all these years of separation and incarceration. She believes him so completely, in fact, that she has turned against her own daughter to support her husband. Do you understand how sure a woman must be of her husband's innocence to side with him over her own child?" the lawyer declares.

I shake my head, trying to remain calm.

"If that alone isn't enough to sell you on Mr.

Smyth's innocence, I don't know what will. Listen, my client has already paid his debt to society, spending years and years behind bars for a crime he did not even commit. Could any of you really, in good conscience, sentence him to remain there any longer? My client deserves a fair trial for once. He deserves to be listened to. He deserves to breathe the free air and walk the streets uninhibited by chains. Will you stand on the right side of history and set him free? Or will you condemn him once again for some other man's crimes? Thank you. That will be all," the lawyer concludes theatrically.

As soon as he is done speaking, I hear a dull roar of activity and whispering in the courtroom audience. So much of it, in fact, that the judge has to bang the gavel to call order once again. And when the tittering dies down to silence again, I can make out a new sound, a strange one that does not seem garbled by static like the rest of it. What is that?

I hurriedly switch off the ham radio and listen intently.

There it is again. A sniffle. A sob. My heart begins to pound as I look around frantically. Somebody is here, cowering in the pitch-black back of the shed. Clutching my gun, I slowly make my way across the shed toward the back, my eyes slowly adjusting to the lack of light. I can make out a small, curled up shadow of a human form near the filthy ground.

No. It can't be.

"Lauren?" I say, the syllables hanging thick in the air.

The sobs turn to a sharp gasp. "Bones?" asks a thin, trembling voice.

"Lauren!" I shout, rushing to her side.

She's hunched over on the ground, shivering and crying. Her face is splotchy with tears and exhaustion, but I would recognize those glorious eyes anywhere, even in the dark. I throw my arms around her and hold her tight, noticing that she feels even more delicate and fragile than she normally does. I feel a flicker of hatred for the man who did this to her. Clearly he hasn't been feeding or taking care of her in the least. Bastard.

"I can't believe it's really you," she whimpers, tears tracking hotly down her cheeks. "I-I never expected anyone to come find me."

"Of course I came to find you," I shoot back passionately. "Lauren, I would not have stopped until I found you. I'm here now. You're safe."

"He... he brought me here. I was so scared. He grabbed me at the beach and I—I couldn't fight back. I tried, Bones, but he got me. God, I'm so stupid," she sighs tearfully.

"No, no. Don't blame yourself," I tell her, cupping her face in both hands. "This is not your fault. A demented excuse for a man did this to you. Come on."

I help her stand up, though she's wobbly on her

feet from stress and starvation. She's not in fantastic condition at the moment, but at least she's no longer alone. "Do you want to get running or should we stick around so I can put a bullet in Kevin's skull?" I ask her.

She bites her lip, thinking it over. Then she says firmly, "No. I don't want to run. I'm done running, Bones. I can't do that anymore. I'm not running from anything from here on out. I'm running to something. You."

I pull her into my arms, stroking her head and kissing the top of her precious, soft head. "Okay, my love. We're going to do this your way," I tell her gently.

I can feel all eyes turning and fixating on the two of us as we walk into the local police station a few towns away. This place is considerably less abandoned-looking than Lauren's hometown, but still rural and off the beaten track. Lauren clearly sees some familiar faces, because she leans into me and squeezes my hand even tighter. A man comes sauntering up to us in uniform, his eyes squinting as though he's trying to place Lauren's face.

"Hello there," he says, blocking our path with his hands on his hips. "What's brought you in today? Can I help you somehow?"

He's asking, but it sounds more like a threat. Lauren is positively quaking next to me, and just as I'm about to speak up on her behalf, the police officer gets a tap on his shoulder from behind. He steps aside to allow a rather short, middle-aged woman with a no-nonsense salt-and-pepper bob and bright, intelligent brown eyes to step forward. I can feel Lauren instantly relax a little as the woman extends a hand—not to shake, but to rest it maternally on her shoulder.

"Raylene?" the woman asks in a low voice.

"It's Lauren now," she whispers back. "Can we... can we talk?"

The woman nods, pointing to her badge proudly. "Yes, dear. We can talk. Do you remember me? I was just a deputy when you came in all those years ago. I'm the Sheriff now."

Lauren's face brightens up and I immediately feel more trusting in this particular cop. I can tell they know each other from way back when, and it dawns on me that this sheriff must have been the one to take Lauren's testimony regarding her father's crimes back when she was still a child. Back when she was called Raylene.

"Is there somewhere quiet we could go? Somewhere private?" I suggest, glancing around at the room full of deputies and cops who are trying to surreptitiously watch us and eavesdrop.

The sheriff nods and gestures for us to follow her. "Sure thing. This way."

Lauren looks up at me and gives a barely-noticeable nod, and we follow the sheriff to a private interview room toward the back of the station. As soon as the door is closed, Lauren bursts into tears. The sheriff hurries to her side, pulling up a chair to sit next to her instead of across the table. That's a good sign, it seems to me. The sheriff sees her as a person, not just a potential stack of boring paperwork. Lauren unloads the full story onto the sheriff, including even the tiniest details. The sheriff and I listen intently as she shares her horrific experiences, and I can see the look on the sheriff's face changing from sympathy to horror to pity. She really seems to care about what Lauren has to say, and she doesn't have a problem with me sitting here holding her hand the whole time. After the story is finished, the sheriff leans back in her chair, shaking her head as she stares down at the woodgrain of the interview table.

"My god, Ray—Lauren. I am so sorry, dear. No one should have to go through what you've been through. You are an amazingly strong, resilient young woman. I applaud you for surviving something that would destroy many people completely," she says, with genuine awe in her voice. "And if it helps at all, I may have some good news to share with you."

"Really?" Lauren sniffles.

"Yes, ma'am," says the sheriff. "Kevin Cranston actually has several warrants out for his arrest. There are charges of harassment, stalking, obstructing justice, hiding evidence, slander, libel—the list goes on and on. He's a career criminal and a bad man. You were right to turn him in, Lauren. Just like you were right to turn in Murray Smyth."

"Thank you. That's really nice to hear," Lauren says softly.

"That's not all," adds the sheriff, a twinkle in her eye. "I'm going to case that shed as soon as we're done here. Full forensics team. The whole nine yards. If there's evidence to be collected, you can bet your bottom dollar we will find it. Oh, and I don't know if you've heard about this yet, but... the results of your father's appeal have come through."

My heart pounds and Lauren squeezes my hand as we wait for the answer.

The sheriff gives us a winning smile. "His appeal was denied. And more than that, they have uncovered new evidence that the judge is allowing to be included. Evidence that we are confident about. It should be enough to put him away for the other three murders."

"That's what they said the first time around," Lauren sighs.

The sheriff pats her on the hand. "I know, dear. But there's new evidence this time that was excluded before. Damning evidence, if I'm being honest. As soon as I caught wind about his new appeal, I reopened the case and discovered new factors we could not have caught the first go around. Forensic technique and technology has improved a lot since you were a little girl, Lauren. It's better now. We're more precise."

"So… you really think it might work?" Lauren says breathlessly.

The sheriff smiles and nods. "Yes, ma'am. We got him. I swear."

After we end the interview, shake hands, and share contact information with the sheriff, she cuts us loose. I walk out into the sunshine with Lauren at my side, hand-in-hand and feeling a million pounds lighter. I look over at her face, shining with happy tears, and can't help but smile.

"So," I begin. "Where do you want to go with your newfound freedom?"

Grinning up at the sun, she says, "I just want to fly away with you."

"Would a ride back to Wyoming on the back of my motorcycle fit the bill?" I ask.

Lauren turns to beam at me, looking more beautiful than ever before with the sun reflecting off her golden hair. "Yes," she agrees warmly. "Even better."

Only once in my life have I been this happy to see the California state line shrinking behind me, and with the wind in my face and the feeling of Lauren's arms around my waist, I have to say, this blows the first time out of the water. We have everything packed, and there's nothing but miles of road and a bright future ahead of us.

Lauren squeezes me as she notices me turn my head to glance in the rear-view mirror, and I chuckle, putting my hand over hers. We're going to have to stop somewhere nice for dinner tonight.

"How long is the ride back to Wyoming?" she shouts over my shoulder.

"Fifteen, sixteen hours," I shout back. "Not counting any time we spend at the hotel rooms I'm getting us."

She presses her face close enough to mine to feel

her smile, and she hugs me tight as I ride. This is why I'm a biker. This is what it's all about. The landscape is whipping by all around me faster than I can keep up with, but at the same time, it stands before me like a vast and unending plain, full of richer beauty than I ever thought possible in the real world. I grew up in a rough town, and I never knew anything else until I was forced to run from it.

But now, we don't have to run from anything. I'm going to take Lauren to new heights in bed at every hotel we stop at, and with the nest-egg I have saved up, I'm going to shell out for the best rooms I can get, while I'm at it.

And once we're back in Wyoming, that's not all I plan on shelling out for, if all goes according to plan. But I can't get ahead of myself.

As the asphalt flies by under my wheels, I notice something in the rear-view mirror. There's a pickup truck behind us, and it looks like it's moving fast. I glance ahead. There's nobody for miles, and it doesn't look like there's anyone behind the truck, either. Thinking little of it, I drive ahead steady. The guy has plenty of room to get around me.

But then I get a bad feeling in my gut.

It's something in the air. The sound of his engine is different than what I'm used to. Spend enough time riding, and you get to know what a truck doing 90-100 miles per hour on the interstate coming up on your left sounds like. This doesn't sound like that. This sounds a little more like it's pushing 140.

"Hold on!" I shout as I tighten my grip on Lauren's hands around my waist and veer to the left as the truck driver hurdles right into where I had been a moment ago.

The fucker is trying to drive us off the road!

I stick my middle finger out as he slams on the brakes so as not to pass me, and when he does, my jaw goes slack when I look into the driver's eyes.

"Kevin?!" Lauren shouts at the punk at the steering wheel.

He's grinning like a crocodile, and he's laughing as he leans on the horn and falls behind us. His face looked sweaty and flushed, and his eyes looked wild. We already know that he has gone off the deep end, but now, he's absolutely crazed...and he's caught up with us.

"How the fuck did he catch us?" I bark as I roar forward, but Kevin is hot on my tail. I reach for my gun, but with Lauren on board, I can't pull the same cowboy shit I used to be able to pull on my own. I'm not going to risk her like that.

In the mirror, I see Kevin take his seatbelt off, and he sticks his head out the window. "Slow down, let's talk it out!" he howls, and as he slinks back into the driver's seat, I can see the cackling grin on his face. The fucker must be strung out on coke, or something.

The truck barrels forward close enough that I can almost *feel* it behind me, and as it starts to back off slowly, I know what's coming. I take my gun out, and I swerve to the opposite side of the road as Kevin guns the ignition and blazes forward. He misses narrowly, and I feel his rear-view mirror come so close to hitting my bicep that I feel the air cutting.

But as the truck hurdles past, I take aim and fire. The bullet hits the door and ricochets off into the plains, but it definitely got Kevin's attention. The fact that it doesn't make him hit the brakes is...troubling. There's a good chance Kevin sees this as the end of the road for him, and if that's true, then he's the most dangerous kind of man there is.

He doesn't have anything to lose.

I take aim again, trying to get a steady shot on one of his tires, but I don't have time to line up the shot—he suddenly swerves in front of me and hits the brakes, screeching abruptly and forcing me to turn the handle hard and go right. I feel the bike start to threaten to spin out on me, and it feels like it takes every muscle in my body to keep me from laying her down and killing us both. Adrenaline pumps through my body like I've never felt it before. I'm not just fighting for me this time, I'm fighting for Lauren and her right to live free from fuckers like this jackass.

And living free is what the Heartbreakers are all

about.

Once my bike is back up, I twist around, extending my gun-toting hand past Lauren to keep her out of the shot and firing. The glass of Kevin's left headlight explodes as it shatters.

"Slow down, I want to talk to him!" Lauren shouts behind me, into my ear.

"What?!" I bark. "He's insane, Lauren! He'll kill us both!"

"You've got a gun!" she reminds me. "If he did, he'd have used it by now!"

"Fuck," I mumble, "you're right. Why?!"

"He's after me," she shouts as Kevin starts to gain on us again. "I might be able to talk him down!"

I glance at Kevin in the mirror, looking at the crazed look on that sweaty face, and I don't think I can see the humanity in him Lauren can. But for her, I'll go out on a limb. I veer left and slow down, holding my barrel up into the air to show that I'm not going to point it at Kevin unless he makes me— and that's a low bar for me.

"Kevin!" Lauren shouts as he glares over at us, looking poised to swerve the truck into us at any second. And truth be told, he probably could—we're almost in a standoff. "Cops are looking for you! It's over!"

"Then two more will be a drop in the bucket!" he barks. "You're gonna fry for what you did to Murray, bitch!"

"You don't even know us!" she hollers, voice cracking as she digs her nails into me. "Why the fuck do you care about Murray?!"

Kevin's head snaps over to us so fast I swear I hear it crack, and his face goes red with anger. "What?!" he shrieks, and I see his right hand lunge for the handbrake.

Several things happen at once on that long, lonely, dusty road.

The second his hand goes down, I have to assume he's reaching for a gun we haven't seen yet. The fact that it turns out to be the handbrake doesn't make a difference as I lower my gun, pointing it as close as I can to his front left tire. Kevin pulls the handbrake at the same time that he yanks the steering wheel left, and suddenly, there's a metal wall of truck closing in around my bike. I pulled the trigger a split second ago, and as I watch Kevin's face come into view, I see his eyes panicked at the sight of his now blown-out tire.

I swing the bike sideways, screeching across the length of the truck...just before its groaning mass of metal tips over from the momentum, missing us so closely that I can catch a half-second of Kevin's scream. His truck starts tumbling over and over off the side of the road, glass shattering and metal bending as it crunches into the desert before getting wedged against a rock and coming to a stop. Miraculously, it lands upright, and a cloud of dust half-obscures it.

"Oh my god," Lauren breathes, eyes wide at the scene.

I'm not letting him go, though. This is beyond personal.

I steer the bike off the road and guide it cautiously down to where Kevin's truck has come to a halt. By the looks of things, it isn't going anywhere anytime soon. My gun is still out, and I still have four good rounds I am not afraid to use.

"Careful," I whisper to Lauren, but she moves around me and rushes forward. "Damnit!"

I run after her, but then I see what she sees: an arm is hanging limply out the window. She rushes to the door and pulls it open, and immediately, Kevin starts to stir, proving that he isn't dead like I thought. Lauren doesn't fail to notice. As he starts to squirm, she reaches into the truck with fire in her eyes and grabs him by the collar, yanking him upright and-

Crack!

"Shit," Lauren curses as Kevin flops to the ground under the impact of the punch Lauren just hit him in the jaw with. The sound of it takes me right back to the night I punched Brandon and first saw Lauren, and I have to admit, it brings a smile to my face despite all this.

Lauren takes a step back as Kevin leans against

his car door while slumped on the ground, breathing heavily and staring up at us as I join her, gun pointed at him.

"Do it," he snaps.

"Shut up," I grunt.

"Why did you do this, Kevin?" Lauren asks, fists still clenched. "My life was already hell. Is this how you get off? Me hurting? Is that just how all you fuckers get off?"

"Maybe that runs in the family," Kevin says with chilling coldness, and Lauren's face pales, bringing a smile to his lips. "He really never told you about me, did he?"

"What?" she breathes, and my eyes widen.

"You think Sandra was the first woman Murray had a child with?" he says, a shaky laugh creeping into his voice. "No. She was just the worst one. Murray had another one, Raylene. He had *me*."

"Holy shit," I murmur as Lauren takes a few quivering steps back, shaking her head.

"What's the matter, sis?" he chuckles up at her, smiling with unnerving calmness. "Disappointed he never invited me over? I was too. I was disappointed when he wouldn't speak to me, too. I was disappointed when he disowned me, and even though I was willing to forgive all that, every *fucking* bit of it, I was disappointed when he wouldn't let me speak to him in prison. Me, the one son of a bitch who fought for him when nobody else would," he snarls, pointing to himself with red-rimmed eyes and a quivering lip. He glares daggers at Lauren, teeth clenched and a trickle of blood running from his nose. "You had a father. You had that life. He *loved* you, Raylene. And you stabbed him in the back."

"You're insane, Kevin," Lauren says, shaking her head slowly. "Even...even if that's true. You have no idea what Murray was like. You didn't see what I saw."

"No!" Kevin barks, and I can see him for the wounded, pathetic child that he is, half-cringing in the dirt. "You didn't have the full picture. You were just a stupid kid! If he had been free, he..."

Kevin's hands ball into fists, and he tears his eyes away from Lauren to look up at me. "Do it, you fucking coward. What are you waiting for?"

"Don't, Bones," Lauren whispers, looking at me with pain in her eyes.

"I was going to kill her," Kevin says, pointing to Lauren and leaning forward. "I still will. I *want* to. Do it! Get it over with!"

But even if Lauren hadn't been urging me not to, I can't bring myself to pull the trigger on the broken soul on the ground before me. We stare each other in the eye long and hard before my ear pricks up. The sounds of sirens in the distance just reached me.

Kevin's head hangs, and he starts to sob as the sirens draw closer, and Lauren slowly slips her arm in mine as I lower my weapon.

His fingertips across my bare flesh feels like fire. Every touch is met with a spiral of intense sensation, blooming bright and hot under my skin. We're lying in a patch of sunlight across the bed in his cabin, where we have been languidly lazing around all morning. These days, it's easier than I ever imagined to just let time tick by. With Bones, the minutes feel like seconds, the hours like minutes, the days passing by in a blink of an eye. I do my best to expand each moment as it unfolds, wringing as much out of every precious second as possible. I am never happier than when we are tangled up together like this, our bodies curling and curving around one another on top of the sheets or underneath them, sharing warmth and blessing each other's skin with soft kisses and fervent, loving touches. He makes me feel safe and wanted, two feelings I never imagined possible for a girl like me. I come from such a dark beginning, and I always assumed that my past would loom over me like a frigid shadow, keeping me in the dark. Alone. Starved for touch and acknowledgement. Desperate for somebody to look at me and see something other than the wispy shell of a woman I felt like.

And I have found that in Bones. He cares for me. Not just on a surface level, but his heart and my heart, together, intertwined forever. I am no longer afraid of the future, because for the first time ever, I feel like I actually have one. I am not alone. I have someone around to laugh and joke around with, someone to share the good and the bad with. Although, I have to admit, there isn't a whole lot of bad left in my life these days.

Quite some time has passed since the day they came and took Cranston away. I was forced to face up to my past, and this time, I had all the weapons and strength I needed to defeat it. Bones inspires me with that strength. He was my spine, my backbone when I felt flimsy and helpless, and now we have spent enough time together that it feels like I have grown my own power. I have learned that I am good enough. Powerful enough to push back against those dark things that haunt me. I have a light in my soul now that shines bright and reduces my demons to mere flickers of shadow. I can turn toward the monster that made me and hold my head up high, no longer afraid of seeing his face reflected in my mirror. He's long since vacated my thoughts. I have other things to think about now. Good things. Hell, I have great things ahead of me, because Bones is walking alongside me in this new life.

Every day, he shows me a new part of myself I never let myself see before. He shows me who I really am, what I am really capable of. And every time he holds me in his arms and entices my body to new heights of pleasure, it's like opening a door previously kept closed and locked. As it turns out, there is so much more to me than where I came from and who made me. I have the choice to determine who I will be from here on out. I have the power to become that version of myself, the version of Lauren that I really like. Bones respects and loves me, and that gives me the key to respect myself, even if I haven't quite learned to love myself yet.

But Bones is working on it, even right now. He will get me there one day. I have no doubt about that. Especially on lazy days like today, watching the dappled light fall over his powerful, muscular body as he turns and moves around with me on the bed. He asks me again and again to trust him, and every time, it gets a little easier. There's a lot of pain to unlearn and heal from, but I'm on my way. And these days, there is far more pleasure in my life than pain.

"God, you're beautiful," he murmurs, propping

himself up on his elbow to peer into my face. I blush and try to turn away reflexively, knowing there isn't a stitch of makeup on my face, and my hair is in need of a wash.

But he doesn't let me turn away. He takes my delicate chin between his thumb and forefinger and gently pulls me back. He gazes deep into my eyes, and I can feel my body heating up instantly. That's all it ever takes nowadays. One look, and I'm mesmerized. At least now I can be sure that I am in safe hands. He slowly bends to kiss me on the lips, his hand sliding over to cup my cheek while his other hand slips down to pull at the hem of my shirt. It's one of his, oversized and well-worn to be softer than before. Sure, I have my own clothes. Plenty of them. Bones and I love to go out to the shops together so he can watch me try on new outfits. Twice now he's come into the dressing room with me, covered my mouth with his hand, and fucked me right there in the store next to a pile of new clothes. Just the memory of that is enough to make me slick between the thighs, and I arch my back to let him pull up the t-shirt, lifting it up over my head. We're going slowly, but I know exactly where we're going. I'm along for the ride, always happy to follow Bones anywhere.

My nipples stiffen to peaks in the cool, free air and I let out a soft moan when Bones lays both hands over my chest. He massages my breasts, rolling my nipples under his thumbs until I'm mewling and rocking my hips, getting frustrated with need.

"Please," I whimper.

"Please, what?" he repeats in a low growl.

"Just… don't stop," I murmur.

He laughs softly and bends to pull one of my nipples between his teeth, biting down gently so that I cry out and writhe beneath him. "Trust me, I don't plan to," he purrs back.

His hands slide up to grasp my wrists, pushing them up over my head. He pins my arms there while his tongue flicks over my nipples, going back and forth between them, every now and then grazing them with his teeth. There's always that glorious edge of gentle pain, of force. Bones loves to test my boundaries, but I love it, too. I know he will only take me to good places. I'm never afraid anymore. I'm just happy to let him do what he pleases— because it pleases *me*.

He reaches up and grabs a bandana from the nightstand. I watch intently as he binds the bandana around my wrists, tying them to a post of the head-board. A little thrill of excitement rolls down my spine as Bones moves to straddle me. He makes his way down slowly, letting his hands and his lips kiss a trail down to my soft mound. He leans in, massaging and squeezing my thighs while he sucks in a deep breath of my fragrant sex. The look of pure hunger on his face is enough to make me tingle all over with anticipation. I never thought I could find someone who so perfectly jives with my light and my darkness at the same time. He lets me explore those once-fearful places deep in my soul, casting light into the shadows, bringing me out into the sunshine even as we delve deeper into my hidden desires. Bones can be hard, but he is always gentle. The bottom line is safety. And trust. And abiding love that conquers all trouble.

I never used to believe in that stuff. But I do now.

Bones spreads apart my thighs and dives in, flicking his tongue up and down my slick flower while my hips roll and buck, the breath holding and catching in my throat. His lips close around my sensitive clit, circling it and sending shockwaves of pure pleasure through my whole body, head to toe. My arms strain above my head as I rut against his tongue, the wetness and warm friction mounting my pleasure ever higher. Bones gets a little more aggressive, licking and sucking at my clit until I'm keening and moaning for release. He knows just how to bring me to the edge and then artfully dance away.

"Oh, you're teasing me," I whisper.

He laughs gently. "Yes. I am. Is that what you deserve?" he growls.

"Maybe," I reply coyly, biting my lip as I open my eyes to look down at him.

He gives me a wry smile and grabs my legs,

hooking them over his shoulders so he can better reach my pussy. He presses the flat, hard tip of his tongue against my clit and circles it slowly, then faster, making big circles and small ones. Just as I'm about to come, he pulls back and spanks my ass—hard. I cry out with mingled pain and pleasure, gushing honey all over his tongue at the new, sharp sensation. I tremble through the orgasm, my hands clenching and unclenching uselessly above my head.

"Good girl. That's what I want," Bones hisses. He dives in and licks up my honey hungrily, his hands still working my thighs.

"More," I beg.

"More? Have you earned more?" he plays with me.

"Yes, sir. Please. I want... I want you inside of me," I murmur.

"You have been a naughty girl lately. The other day, when you were cooking dinner, I know you know I could see right through those pale pink panties. I saw you getting wet. You were thinking about my cock, weren't you? You were thinking about me bending you over that kitchen sink and fucking you from behind again," he snarls.

I bite my lip, blushing bright pink. He's right. As always.

"Guilty," I admit.

"No reason to feel guilty," he murmurs. "If you

want my cock, you're going to get it. Hard." He sits up and slaps my ass again with a resounding smack.

It stings so deliciously that I'm still floating on cloud nine when I see him pull down his boxers and let his cock spring free. I lick my lips, hungry for it. He's already stiff and hard for me as he rubs the head of his cock around my slick opening. I rut against him, moaning and pleading for him to take me.

"You want it bad, little girl?" he says in a rasping voice.

"Yes. God, yes," I gasp, bracing myself for the inevitable. I've been hungry for it all day.

With that, he pushes inside of me, totally sheathing himself inside my clenching cunny. I cry out and buck against him, both of us rolling and thrusting in perfect tandem. The swollen head of his cock brushes against my g-spot again and again, and it's not long before I come again, gushing all over his massive shaft as he pummels my pussy. I lose myself to the waves of pleasure, groaning and rocking in rhythm with him as he fucks me hard and fast. He reaches up to gently pull my hair, turning my head to one side so he can kiss and bite at my neck while he slams into me. He moves faster, fucking me so deeply that I know I'll be sore the rest of the day. Tomorrow, too. But I live for this—for the moments when he truly lets go and uses my body the way he needs to. I belong to him and I love it when he marks me up, makes it clear exactly who I belong to.

I love feeling the marks he's left, seeing the reminders that he has been there, like a road map on my body of special places.

"You feel so damn good, sweetheart," he purrs against my ear, sending shivers down my spine. I rise to meet his every crest, moaning as we move toward climax together.

He strokes my face, showing how soft he can be even as he pounds hard into my pussy, his other hand groping my breasts and feeling me up. We hurtle toward the edge, slipping closer and closer until finally he picks up the pace and pummels into me a few more times, and we explode as one being, gasping and groaning with pleasure. I love the feeling of his come inside me, pumping me full and making me feel complete. He gives me a few more short thrusts and then he withdraws, kissing me all over my face and body before untying my hands.

We curl up together and he strokes my cheek, our eyes locked on one another's gaze.

"So, my love," he whispers, "what do you want to do today?"

I smile playfully and reply, "What's wrong with what we're doing now?"

He chuckles and kisses my forehead. "Nothing at all. But first, I'm going to make some breakfast." I immediately try to get up, but he stops me. "No—you stay right there. I'm going to bring it to you," he explains.

I smile, shaking my head at how lucky I am as he walks out of the room. I lie in the sunshine, relaxing and feeling his come slowly drip down my thighs as I listen to Bones humming in the kitchen. My phone buzzes on the nightstand and, though I toy with the idea of ignoring it, my curiosity overcomes me and I grab it, sliding the screen open. There's a news alert that makes my heart skip a beat. I see his name: Murray Smyth. But then, the headline clicks in my mind.

He's been arrested and charged with the murders of three girls many years ago. Thank god there's no statute of limitations on murder. I smile to myself, knowing he couldn't outrun his own past, either. And then, as a footnote to the article about my father, there's a link to another article. I scan the page and feel my soul get ten times lighter when I learn that Kevin Cranston has been arrested and charged for stalking and kidnapping. I know I'm going to have to take the stand again. It's going to be a little scary. How could it not be? But this time, it'll be different. I won't be alone. I have Bones now, always in my corner, ready to protect and defend me. And it's not just him, either. The Heartbreakers are all on my side, too. They are my new family.

All my monsters, neatly contained somewhere far away from me. It's a dream come true. A day I never thought would come. And all I can do is smile.

My phone rings again and I pick it up without

even checking the caller ID. I don't have to do that anymore. There's no fear. Only openness to the beautiful future unfolding before me.

"Hello?" I answer, turning over on my side.

"Lauren! Hey, it's Kate," says a cheery voice.

I grin. "Oh, hey! How's it going?" I reply.

She carries on chattering about the baby, about Breaker. About how happy she is, how good things are. I feel exactly the same way. And it's strange—I never knew how good it could feel to have a best friend, but I have one now. We talk nearly every day. As it turns out, Kate and I have a lot in common. As we chat, it's hard for me not to let sip that I've been planning her baby shower. I'm so excited for us girls to gather up and celebrate the new life coming into the world. A new member of our extended but tight-knit family. We talk for a while as Bones cooks breakfast, but when he comes in and sets a tray on my lap in bed, I have to hang up.

"Blueberry pancakes?" I ask, looking up at him.

He nods. "Your favorite, right?"

I grin at him happily. "Absolutely."

"Well, dig in," he says, sitting down next to me.

"Don't have to tell me twice," I giggle, picking up my fork. I reach to lift the napkin and set it in my lap, but then I do a double take. There's something there, under the napkin. Something sparkly and shiny.

A ring.

My heart begins to pound as I pick it up gingerly, my eyes wide when I turn to look at Bones. There's a big, gorgeous smile on his handsome face that takes my breath away.

"Is this…?" I trail off breathlessly.

He nods, leaning in and kissing me on the lips gently. He strokes the hair back out of my face, beaming at me. "I want you to always have a physical reminder of my love for you. Lauren, I intend to spend every day for the rest of our lives taking care of you and defending you. I will always keep you safe. Remember that. You are mine, and I am yours. I love you. I always will," he says warmly. There's so much pure adoration in his gaze, I can feel my heart melting.

"I love you, too," I murmur, happy tears burning in my eyes. "Now and forever."

Trafficked

Stealing Her

The Assassin's Heart

Killing For Her

Abducted

KILLERS:

Hunter's Baby

I Hired A Hitman

STEPBROTHERS:

Ruthless

Criminal

GLITZ & GRIT:

Betting on Love

Vegas Boss

Rock Hard Bodyguard

Innocence For Sale: Jane

Redeeming Viktor

SEXY SEALs

Sweetheart for the SEAL

Sights on the SEAL

Romance:

Falling for her Boss (Novella)

Most Wanted: Lilly (Novella)

Bound as the World Burns (SFF)

<u>**Erotic Thriller:**</u>

THE DANGEROUS MEN SERIES:

The Narrow Path

Strayed from the Path

Path to Ruin

ABOUT THE AUTHOR

Alexis Abbott is a Wall Street Journal & USA Today bestselling author who writes about bad boys protecting their girls! Pick up her books today if you can't resist a bad boy who is a good man, and find your-self transported with super steamy sex, gritty suspense, and lots of romance.

She lives in beautiful St. John's, NL, Canada with her amazing husband.

facebook.com/abbottauthor

twitter.com/abbottauthor

instagram.com/alexisabbottauthor

bookbub.com/authors/alexis-abbott

pinterest.com/badboyromance

youtube.com/AlexisAbbott

ACKNOWLEDGMENTS

Thank you to my amazing Patrons. I'm constantly humbled and grateful for your support.

Ramona Cabrera
Melissa Hedrick
Virginia Swanson
Dawn Daughenbaugh
Don Doss
Stacie Currie

If you'd like to join them — and get my ebooks or paperbacks — you can find me here on Patreon. https://www.patreon.com/alexisabbott